Kim Lawrence lives on a farm in Anglesey with her university-lecturer husband, assorted pets who arrived as strays and never left, and sometimes one or both of her boomerang sons. When she's not writing, she loves to be outdoors gardening or walking on one of the beaches for which the island is famous—along with being the place where Prince William and Catherine made their first home!

Books by Kim Lawrence

Harlequin Presents

Beauty and the Greek
The Price of Scandal
Captivated by Her Innocence
One Night with Morelli
Surrendering to the Italian's Command
A Ring to Secure His Crown
The Greek's Ultimate Conquest

One Night With Consequences

Her Nine Month Confession

Wedlocked!

One Night to Wedding Vows

Visit the Author Profile page at Harlequin.com for more titles.

Kim Lawrence

A CINDERELLA FOR THE DESERT KING

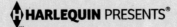

HARLEQUIN PRESENTS®

Recycling programs
for this product may
not exist in your area.

ISBN-13: 978-1-335-50461-6

A Cinderella for the Desert King

First North American publication 2018

Copyright © 2018 by Kim Lawrence

Printed in U.S.A.

A CINDERELLA FOR
THE DESERT KING

For Herb, my much-missed writing companion
and friend—best dog ever!

CHAPTER ONE

ABBY FOSTER WAS HOT, her feet ached—part of the photo shoot had involved her walking up a sand hill in shorts and four-inch heels—and something had bitten her on the arm. The thick layer of make-up had disguised it but not stopped it throbbing and itching like hell.

All that was bad enough but what was *really* the icing on the cake was the fact that their transport had broken down. She'd been meant to be in the first four-wheel drive, the one she had travelled out of Aarifa city to their desert location in, but the stylist had pushed past her, bagging a seat next to the photographer's assistant the girl had a crush on.

So, thanks to young love, Abby was now stranded in the middle of who knew where, trying without success to tune out the raised, angry voices outside. So far she had resisted the urge to add her own voice to the melee, but her clenched teeth were beginning to ache with the effort.

Leave well alone remained the best strategy, though, so along with Rob, who had reacted to being stranded in a desert by promptly taking the opportunity to grab a nap and falling asleep, she'd waited inside the broken-down vehicle.

It was a decision she was starting to rethink as the temperature inside the dark car rose and Rob, the person who had made her climb that damned sand dune ten times before he was satisfied he'd got the shot, began to snore.

Loudly!

Rolling her eyes, she pulled a bottle of water from the capacious tote bag she always carried with her. Despite the frequent-traveller miles she had clocked up since she'd embarked on her modelling career, Abby had never mastered the art of travelling light.

She had half-unscrewed the top before caution kicked in and she realised she may need to ration herself. Before he'd fallen asleep Rob had confidently claimed they would be rescued in a matter of minutes, but what if the photographer was being overly optimistic?

What if they were stuck here longer?

The internal debate didn't last long. Her

grandparents had raised her to always be cautious—pity they hadn't displayed the same quality when it came to financial advice, considering they'd been swindled out of their life savings by a crooked financial advisor. But caution won out.

Gregory's good-looking face, complete with that boyishly sincere smile, materialised in her head as she tightened the lid with a vicious turn and put the bottle back into her bag. Her jaw clenched, she fought her way through the familiar toxic mixture of guilt and self-contempt she experienced whenever she considered her own part in her grandparents' situation. They put a brave face on it but she knew how unhappy they were.

It didn't matter which way you looked at it, it *was* her fault Nana and Pops had lost their financial security.

If *she* hadn't been fool enough to fall for Gregory's sincere smile and the blue eyes that went with it, and if *she* hadn't imagined herself in love and taken the sweet man of her dreams home to meet her grandparents, then they would still have the comfortable retirement they had worked so hard for to look forward to.

Instead they had nothing.

Her throat thickened with emotion, which she dismissed with a tiny impatient shake of her head. Tears, she reminded herself, weren't going to fix anything; what she needed was a plan.

And she had one. At last.

A militant gleam lit her green eyes as her rounded chin lifted to a determined angle. By her calculations, if she took every single piece of work that came her way—barring those that wanted her to pose minus clothes, and there were quite a few—in another eighteen months she'd be able to buy back the retirement bungalow her grandparents had lost because of her conman boyfriend. She'd brought him into their lives, he'd got them all to trust him and then he had vanished with her grandparents' life savings. In a vicious parting shot he'd emailed her a photo of him with another man, the pose they were in making the salt-in-the-wound footnote 'You're not really my type' slightly redundant.

Gregory's *patience* with her inexperience and his reassurance that he was prepared to wait because he respected her now made perfect sense.

Shutting out the humiliating memories before they took hold, Abby peeled off a wet wipe from a packet in the inner pocket of her bag. Eyes closed, she wiped her face and neck, removing the last of her make-up along with some of the dust and grime.

She was repeating the action while thinking longingly of a cool shower and a cold beer when one of the two men outside put his head into the cab. He fiddled with something beside the steering wheel before turning reproachfully to Abby.

'You might have said something, Abby—we've been trying to open the damned engine for hours.' He gave the lever he'd located a sharp tug and yelled to the man outside. 'Got it, Jez!'

By her count it had actually only been ten minutes. 'It felt more like days,' she retorted, more bothered by the swelling bite on her arm than defending herself from this unfair criticism. Teeth gritted, she rolled up the sleeve of her blouse to take the pressure off the area, not that the shirt was actually *hers*—she was still wearing the outfit selected for today's shoot, the shorts and shirt apparently meant to convince viewers that if a girl chose the new shampoo the company was unveiling with this campaign, they too could go from a casino table to trekking up sand dunes in the desert all while maintaining perfect, glowing hair. They might, but they'd also have blisters if they wore these wretched heels.

The developments through the fly-speckled window didn't look good. The men had both stepped back hastily from the scalding steam that billowed out from the engine.

And then they both started shouting again.

She nudged Rob's foot with her own—luckily for him she had swapped the spiky heels for canvas pumps.

'We should go out and see if we can help.'

Or at least stop them killing one another, she thought as she grabbed a scarf from her bag and pulled the strands of sweat-damp hair back from her face, securing the flaming waves at her nape in a ponytail that was neither smooth nor elegant.

As she got to her feet, head down to avoid banging it on the door frame, Rob opened one eye, nodded, then closed it again and began to quietly snore.

Cool was the wrong word, but at least the temperature outside was marginally less oppressive than that inside the car.

'So, what's the verdict, guys?' she asked, adopting a cheerful tone.

Her attitude did not rub off on the two men.

On the occasions she had worked with the lighting technician previously, Jez had always had a joke up his sleeve to lighten tense situations, but his sense of humour had clearly deserted him today. Frowning heavily, he stepped away from the inner workings of the steaming engine, his face glistening with sweat as he dropped the bonnet back into place.

'It won't go and, before anyone asks, I haven't got a clue what's wrong or how to fix it. If anyone else feels the urge…be my guest.' The thickset technician tossed a challenging look in the direction of the younger man but the intern's aggression had drained away and he was standing biting his nails, suddenly looking very young and very scared.

'No need to worry, Jez. I'm sure once they realise they've left us behind they'll come back to look for us,' Abby said, determined to look on the bright side, despite the fact that the sun was quickly setting and darkness was starting to steal across the desert around them.

'We shouldn't have stopped,' the younger man muttered under his breath as he kicked a tyre.

The older man nodded his agreement. 'What's *he* doing?' He nodded towards the vehicle where the self-acknowledged photographic genius lay sleeping, exhausted, presumably by the effort of taking several dozen shots of an unusually shaped rock with a lizard sitting on it. By the time he had been satisfied with the result, the two lead vehicles in their small convoy had vanished back towards the city they'd come from earlier in the day.

'He's asleep.'

Abby's announcement was greeted with astonished looks and a cry in unison. *'Un-bloody-believable!'*

The two men looked at one another and laughed, their mutual disgust for Rob draining some of the hostility out of the situation. The smiles didn't last long though.

'Anyone got a phone signal?'

Abby shook her head. 'Well, what's the worst that could happen?'

'We die a slow and painful death from thirst?' Rob's voice suddenly cut in as he made a graceful and yawn-filled ascent from the vehicle.

Abby threw him a look. 'Seriously, what *is* the worst that can happen? At least we'll have a story to tell over dinner when we get home.'

'Guys.'

They all turned to look at Jez, who grinned broadly as he stabbed a finger towards plumes of dust in the distance. 'They've come back for us!'

Abby sighed and wiped the moisture from her forehead. 'Thank God!' She frowned at the sound coming from the direction of the fast-approaching vehicles. 'What was that?'

The young man shook his head, looking as puzzled as Abby felt. The two older men exchanged sharp glances, Rob turning to her. 'Maybe you should get back inside, Abby, love.'

'But—' This time the sharp cracking noises were louder and Abby felt her initial relief at being found slip away, replaced by the first flurries of fear as she stared at the approaching dust cloud. 'Was that gunfire?' she whispered.

'We're fine,' Jez said, shading his eyes. 'We're in Aarifa… It's safe as houses. Everyone knows that.' Another volley of gunfire cut across his words. He glanced at Abby. 'Maybe just to be on the safe side you should go inside and keep your head down…?'

The pure-bred Arab horse picked his sure-footed way through a darkness that was profound, a thick, velvety blackness against which the flowing white robe of his rider stood out. Rider and animal, at full gallop, moved in harmony across the sand, slowing only when they reached the first rocky outcrop. At a distance, the column of rock seemed to rise vertically from the ground, but in reality the spiralling path to the summit, though not one recommended to someone without a head for heights, was a series of shorter ascents punctuated by relatively flat sections.

The highly bred horse was panting by the time they crested the summit and paused, the animal drawing air through flared nostrils, the rider waiting for the usual sense of peace this spot gave him.

Not tonight though.

Tonight, even the three-hundred-and-sixty-degree panorama—incredible any time of day but especially magnificent at night, set against the backdrop of a velvet sky sprinkled with stars—failed to penetrate or lift Zain Al Seif's black mood. The most he could claim was the relaxing of a little of the tension in his muscles as he drank in the view, the illuminated ancient walls of the palace with its towers and spires making it visible for miles around. Tonight, however, there were more lights than usual, lights that spread into the old town, built within the shadow of the citadel walls and extended beyond into a geometric pattern created by the brightly illuminated tree-lined boulevards of the modern city with its tall, glass-fronted buildings.

There were a *lot* more lights tonight because today the city…the whole country, in fact… was celebrating. There had been a wedding. A *royal* wedding.

And the world loved a royal wedding, Zain reflected, his sensually sculpted lips twitching into a cynical curve. On this occasion, the world minus one.

He couldn't escape it even here.

The horse responded to Zain's tight-lipped curse with a snort that was loud in the stillness. His mount, picking up on his own mood, began to paw the ground and dance around in circles that would have sent a less experienced rider catapulting over his head.

'Sorry, boy…' Zain soothed, patting the spooked animal's neck, an action that sent out a puff of the red dust that clung to everything in this desert. He waited for his horse to calm down before dismounting, an action he performed in one supple, well-practised action, his boots making no sound as he landed lightly on the uneven stone surface.

Releasing the reins, he took two steps forward and stood on the edge, not noticing the dizzying drop into blackness as his deep-set electric-blue eyes were drawn to the city's lights. As he stared the faint smile that had curved his lips disappeared, those same lips flattening into a grim line. His dark, angled brows drew together in a parallel line above his hawkish, narrow nose as he embraced a fresh surge of self-contempt.

He deserved to feel like a fool, because he had *been* a fool. A complacent bloody fool.

Yes, he'd had a lucky escape but that was the problem—he'd needed luck. He prided himself on being such a great judge of people but the beautiful bride being toasted by an entire country and assorted foreign dignitaries had totally fooled him with her act. The only positive he could see in the situation was that his heart had not been involved. His pride, however, was another matter and it had taken a serious hit.

Of course, *now* Zain could see the clues, but during the pleasurable six-month affair he had remained oblivious even when he had crossed his own self-imposed very clear line; the progress towards it had been so insidious he hadn't heard the alarm bells when he had started thinking of what they shared as a *relationship*… Who knew where that could have led?

Luckily, he never had to find out, because Kayla had got tired of playing the waiting game and when she received a better offer she took it. Zain, still under the illusion they were playing by *his* rules, had never for a moment suspected that lovely…lovely, *poisonous* Kayla had been playing him.

She had turned up at his apartment in Paris earlier than expected after her trip home to Aarifa to see her family. He'd been pleased enough to rearrange his schedule so they could spend the afternoon in bed. Afterwards, as he lay in bed, his attention was divided between the laptop propped on his knees and Kayla, who had dressed before taking a seat in front of the mirror and beginning to repair her make-up.

'You really don't need that,' he'd said offhandedly.

They had been enjoying a discreet affair for six months and he had never seen her without her make-up. On the admittedly few occasions they had spent the night together she always vanished to the bathroom before he woke, emerging looking flawless, a silent signal there would be no repeat performance that morning as she didn't want her hair mussed or her lipstick smudged.

She had turned to him at his words, lipstick in hand and a hardness in her smile he had not seen before. 'Sweet of you to say but,' she paused and applied a second layer of red to her lips before standing up and strolling back to the bed, 'although I was prepared to pretend to like art and opera and even be interested in supremely boring politics for you, I've never been prepared to settle for the fresh-faced look you seem to like in your women.'

The shrillness in her laugh had made him wince, so unlike her usual placating style designed to stroke his ego.

'No-strings-attached sex...did you *really* believe that was all I wanted? Do you *really* think we met by accident, that I took that awful pittance-paying art-gallery job because I want a career? Oh, well, at least it wasn't a complete loss. I certainly never had to pretend with you when we were in bed...' The concession emerged on a deep sigh. 'You know, I'm really going to miss this.'

Zain, still processing the contents of her confession, had not yet reacted as she sat down on the edge of the bed and trailed a red fingernail down his bare, hair-roughened chest, but his lips curled in distaste now at the memory.

'I thought I owed you…' she paused '…well, nothing actually, but I figured one more time, for old times' sake, wouldn't hurt. My family are formally announcing my engagement to your brother next weekend, so I'm afraid, darling, we won't be able to do this for a while. Don't look so shocked! It is kind of your fault. All I ask is that you try and look a teeny bit heartbroken at the wedding. It would make your brother's day.'

Now, alone in the desert, Zain felt his lips curl into a thin-lipped smile. He might not have inherited his father's physical characteristics but it seemed that he had inherited a genetic predisposition to be blind to women's faults. Then the smile vanished as he scanned the moon-silvered landscape and pushed away the self-contempt.

Acknowledging a weakness meant you could guard against it.

His father had lived the last fifteen years of his life consumed by a combination of self-pity and pathetic hope, not accepting the reality of a situation. It had been the man's downfall.

It would *not* be Zain's.

He stared out into the darkness as the scene

in his head continued to replay with relentless accuracy.

'Of course, I'd prefer to marry you, darling, but you never did ask, did you?' Kayla had reproached with a pout, the truth of her anger showing for the first time. 'And I put *so* much effort into being perfect for you. Still, once things have settled we can pick up where we left off in bed, at least, so long as we're discreet. And that's the beauty of it all—Khalid isn't…well, let's just say he's in no position to object, as I have enough dirt on him to…'

Zain abruptly closed down the conversation playing in his head.

People wrote bucket lists of things they wanted to do before they died. At nine, practical Zain had penned a list of things he would *never* do while he lived. Over the years, some had fallen by the wayside—he'd actually grown quite fond of green vegetables, and kissing girls had proved less awful than he'd thought—but others he had rigidly stuck to. The primary one being that he would never allow himself to fall in love or get married—he was determined never to repeat the mistakes his father had made.

Marriage and love had not only broken his proud father as a man but also had threatened the stability of the country he ruled and the people he owed a duty to. Watching the process as a youngster, Zain had been helpless to do anything, the love and respect he once felt for his father turning to anger and shame.

The situation could have had more serious consequences—not that his father would have cared—had the sheikh not been surrounded by a circle of courtiers and advisors loyal to him. Somehow, they had shielded him and managed to maintain the illusion of the strong, wise ruler for the people.

Zain had not been shielded.

He shook his head, aware that he was indulging in a pastime that he would have been the first to condemn in others, and he didn't tolerate those who lived in the past.

A movement in the periphery of his vision interrupted his stream of thought.

Head inclined in a listening attitude, Zain turned his head and stared hard through the dark towards where the invisible border between Aarifa and their neighbour Nezen lay.

He was on the point of turning away, deciding he'd imagined it, when suddenly it was there again…a flash of light that could be a flashlight, or possibly headlights. The light was accompanied this time by a distant sound that drifted across the moonlit emptiness… It sounded like voices shouting.

This time, lights stayed on. Definitely headlights.

He sighed, feeling little enthusiasm for rescuing what would inevitably turn out to be some damn idiot tourist—they averaged about ten a month—with no respect for the elemental environment. Zain loved the desert but he also had a healthy respect for the dangers it presented.

He sometimes wondered if the deep emotional connection he felt with the land of his birth was made stronger by the fact that, growing up an interloper, he'd had to prove his right to belong.

Things had changed, though sometimes an overheard comment or knowing glance would make him wonder just how much.

Admittedly, no one called him names these days, no gangs egged on by his brother threw stones, excluded him or simply beat him up, but scratch the surface and the prejudices were still there. His existence continued to be an insult to many in the country, especially those members of the leading Aarifan families.

He was more of an annoyance than his mother, who at least was living on another continent. It would have been easier in many ways if he had been a bastard, but his parents had married, not letting a little thing like his father's already having a wife and an heir get in the way of true love.

Love...!

A growing noise of distaste vibrated in his throat as, with a creak of leather, he heaved himself back into the saddle and turned the horse. That word again. In his mind it was hard to be sane and celebrate something that people over the centuries used to justify...well, pretty much anything from bad choices to full-scale war!

Love really was the ultimate in selfishness.

He didn't have to look much farther than his own parents to see its destructive power—there was no doubt of his father's enduring love for his mother, but it was as if their love story had been perfectly designed to increase tabloid turnover.

The sheikh of a wealthy middle-eastern state—married to a wife who had already given him an heir—had fallen for the tempestuous Italian superstar of the opera world, a diva in every sense of the word... Zain's mother.

Despite its progressive reputation, setting

aside a wife was not unheard of in Aarifa—in fact, there were circumstances, even in these more enlightened times, when it would be positively encouraged, and even by the discarded bride's family if brought on by the need for a male heir, especially when that heir would one day be the country's ruler.

But Zain's father had already had an heir and the wife whom he dishonoured by setting her aside came from one of the most powerful families in the country. The humiliation of the sheikh's betrayal of the family with impeccable lineage was compounded by the unsuitability of the bride Sheikh Aban al Seif took in her stead, and the fact that the unsuitable bride had won over all her critics with her charm and smiles.

A nation had loved her and then fell dramatically out of love with her when she had walked away from her husband and eight-year-old son to resume her career.

The irony was that her humiliated, proud husband, the leader who had never dodged making tough decisions, the man known for his strength and determination, had not fallen out of love despite her betrayal. He'd have taken her back in a heartbeat and both his sons knew this, which perhaps accounted for the fact that they had never been what anyone could term *close*.

And in many ways, just like their father, Khalid was stuck in the past. His eyes still shone with pure malice when he looked at the half-brother whom he still held responsible for every bad thing that had happened to him and his mother. He still wanted whatever Zain had, be it success, accolades or, now, the woman on his arm. Ultimately it was about depriving not possessing and, once he had whatever it was he coveted from Zain, Khalid usually lost interest.

Would he lose interest in Kayla now he had her?

Zain shrugged to himself in the darkness. It was no longer his concern.

CHAPTER TWO

Zain had covered half the distance to the stranded vehicle when he came across signs that made him slow, stop and, after circling, finally dismount to investigate.

He lost the attitude of disgruntled resignation with which he had embarked on the task as he studied the impressions of tyre tracks that stood out, dark in the moonlight. He picked up one of the shell casings that littered the area, holding it in the palm of his hand for a moment before flinging it away and leaping back into the saddle.

It took him ten minutes before he reached the car that stood with its headlights blazing. He yelled out a couple of times before the three men hiding inside revealed themselves, the drift of the hissed exchange between them suggesting to Zain that his ability to speak English without an accent made him friend not foe in their eyes.

Having halted the garbled explanations they all started to share, he demanded they speak one at a time and he listened, struggling to hold his tongue as he heard them describe what was a list of ineptitude that was in his mind approaching criminal, but there was a limit to his restraint.

'You had a woman with you, out here?' He could not hide his contempt.

'We didn't plan to get stranded, mate,' the older man, who was nursing a black eye, said defensively. 'And we told Abby to hide inside the cab when that mob drove up, but when they started laying into Rob,' he nodded towards the taller man and Zain noticed the wound on his hairline that was still seeping blood, 'she jumped out and laid into the guy with—'

'It was her bag. She hit him with it.'

'And then they hit her back.'

'Was she conscious when they took her?'

It was the oldest man who responded to the terse question. 'I'm not sure but she didn't move when they chucked her in the back.'

The youngest, who looked little more than a boy to Zain's eyes, began to weep. 'What will they do to her… Abby, what will they do to Abby?' he wailed.

The older man laid a hand on his shoulder.

'She'll be all right, son. You know Abby—she's tough, and she can talk her way out of anything. She'll be all right, won't she?' he repeated, throwing a look of appeal at Zain.

Zain saw no need to wrap up the truth. 'They'll keep her alive until they've assessed whether she's worth money.' It had been two years since the last border raids from Nezen. His father's defence minister, Said, would be alarmed when he heard about this new incursion by the criminal gangs who lived in the foothills.

The brutal pronouncement drew a strangled sob from the boy.

What happens if I die here—who will pay off Nana and Pops's debts? You're not going to die, Abby. Think!

She lifted her chin and blinked, flinching as the yelling men riding up and down on camels fired off another volley of bullets into the air.

She'd lost consciousness when they'd thrown her in the truck and when she'd come to she'd had a sack over her head—a situation that had escalated her fear and sense of disorientation to another frantic level. What time was it? Where was she and what was going to happen next?

She still didn't know the answer to either question and she wasn't sure she wanted to know any longer.

She stiffened, her nostrils flaring in distaste as one of the men grabbed her hair in his filthy hand and tugged her towards him to leer in her face. She stared stonily ahead, only breathing again once he had let her go and moved away.

Ignoring the panic she could feel lapping at the edge of her resolve, she lifted her chin. *Think, Abby. Think.*

The effort to make her brain work felt like trying to run in sand, an apt analogy considering that the gritty stuff coated everything.

She clenched her jaw and ignored the pain in her cheek from where one of her captors had casually backhanded her when she'd tried to stop them beating Rob. She had to work out what she was going to do and how much time she had lost while she was blacked out. It seemed like another lifetime that the jeeps loaded with men wielding guns had surrounded their broken-down four-wheel-drive but it couldn't have been that long ago.

It was still dark but the surrounding area was lit up not just by a massive bonfire, which was throwing out enough heat to slick her body in sweat, but also by the headlights of upwards of twenty or so cars and trucks parked haphazardly, enclosing the dusty area on three sides.

She pulled surreptitiously on the rope around her wrists but they held tight. Though her feet were unbounded and she was tempted to run, she doubted she'd get far. It would take only seconds for the half a dozen whooping men who rode back and forth on camels to catch her.

And where would she go?

There were no women.

Abby had never felt more isolated and afraid in her life. She had never known it was *possible* to feel this scared, but, though initially the fear had made her brain freeze, it began to work with feverish speed and clarity as one of the men who had dumped her down came across and said something in a harsh voice.

She shook her head to indicate she didn't understand but he shouted again, and then when she didn't react he bent forward and dragged her to her feet, pushing her forward until they reached an area where a dozen or so of the men were gathered in a half-circle.

When she pulled away from the group the man towing her pushed her hard in the small of her back and produced a long, curved, wicked-looking dagger. Expecting the worst, she fought against tears as he pulled her arms.

Then the tears fell—partly in relief and partly in pain—as he sliced through the cord that held her hands behind her back.

She was rubbing her aching wrists when he began to speak, addressing the men gathered around and pointing at her. Someone shouted something and he grabbed her hair, holding it up to the firelight and drawing a gasp from the men with greedy eyes all fixed on her.

She cringed inwardly, her skin crawling at the touch of the eyes moving over her body. Desperately conscious of her bare legs, she wanted to pretend this wasn't really happening to her, but it was. The sense of helplessness boiled over as she stood, hands clenched stiffly at her sides, shaking from a combination of gut-clenching fear and anger.

The man beside her spoke again, and as other yells echoed in answer she realised what was happening—she was being auctioned off to the highest bidder.

Outrage and horror clenched in her as she began to shake her head, trying to yell out and tell them that they couldn't do this. But the words shrivelled in her throat, her vocal cords literally paralysed with fear.

She closed her eyes to shut out the nightmare of the leering faces, opening them in shock when the man beside her tore open her blouse to the sound of applause from the watching men as it gaped, revealing her bra.

Anger pierced the veil of fear and spurred Abby into retaliatory action. She didn't pause to consider the consequences of her actions, she just lifted a clenched fist and swung. The man moved at the last moment but she caught his shoulder with a hard blow that drew a grunt of pain from him.

Someone laughed and the initial look of open-mouthed shock on his face morphed into something much uglier. There was no point running. There was nowhere to run *to*. The determination not to show her fear was suddenly stronger than the fear itself and Abby lifted her chin, clinging to her pride as she drew the tattered shreds of her shirt tightly around her against the imminent threat. The man advanced towards her, snarling angry words she didn't understand, not that a dictionary was needed when his intent was pretty clear.

He lifted a hand to strike her when suddenly he froze. Everyone did, as a horse with a robed rider galloped full pelt into the semicircle, causing chaos as the men threw themselves to one side to avoid the slashing hooves. Just when it seemed as if man and horse were about to gallop straight into the flames of the bonfire, the horse stopped dead.

The rider, having achieved the sort of theatre-hushed entrance that film directors would have traded a row of awards for, calmly looked around, taking his time and not seeming to be bothered by the guns aimed at him.

After a moment, he loosed the reins and let them fall. The animal didn't move an inch as his rider casually vaulted to the ground, projecting a mixture of arrogance and contempt.

Any idea that the hauteur and arrogance he oozed had anything to do with his superior position on the impressive animal vanished since, if anything, his air of command was even more pronounced as he began to move with long-legged purpose towards the spot where Abby stood as transfixed as everyone else by the tall figure in the flowing white robes. His elegance liberally coated his every move, oozing a level of undiluted male sexuality that had nothing to do with the way he was dressed or even the fact that, even without the dusty riding boots he wore, he had to be at least six foot six, with the length of leg and width of shoulders to carry off the height.

The rest of the men present wore Arab dress but there the similarity ended. The dregs of humanity who had been part of this degrading scene were bedraggled specimens. This man was...*magnificent.*

Abby registered this fact while not losing sight of the truth that he was probably just as much of a threat to her...maybe even more so. She ought not to care about such things in her position, but his face had perfectly sculpted features, symmetrical angles and hollows so dramatically beautiful that she experienced an almost visceral thrill of awareness looking at him.

He held the eyes of the man beside her until the man lowered his arm. The stranger gave a curt nod and then his gaze moved on to Abby. His scrutiny lacked the leering quality of the other mens' but it was equally disturbing, though in an entirely different way. Her tummy fluttered erratically in reaction to his blue-eyed stare.

She lifted her chin and planted her hands on her hips, staring right back until a draught made her realise that her ripped blouse was still displaying a lot of skin. Head bent, cheeks hot, she clumsily attempted to pull the sides closer together across her chest as she awkwardly fastened the buttons with shaking fingers. The top button had gone so she used the one below and, as it was either cover her breast or her midriff, she chose her breast.

She thought she might have imagined the flicker of something close to admiration in the horseman's lean face before he turned and spoke to the man who appeared to be the auctioneer.

His voice was low, a throaty, abrasive quality giving the deep, velvet drawl texture.

Whatever he said caused one of the men who had been bidding to step forward, shouting and gesticulating in protest. As the shouting man reached Abby she leaned back, her nostrils flaring in distaste as his foul breath wafted over her face. She winced and closed her eyes as he grabbed her hair, steeling herself against the pain she anticipated. But it never came.

Instead, the man's grip loosened and fell away, the stench receding. Head bent, she half-opened her eyes and saw the man who had grabbed her standing some feet away. He was still close but his focus was not on her, it was on the tall, white-clad figure who stood smiling with his hand curled around the man's upper arm, seemingly oblivious to the wicked-looking blade pointed at him.

Abby held her breath, her heart continuing to fling itself against her ribcage with bone-cracking force, while this fresh top-up to the adrenaline already flowing through her veins made her head spin.

She felt strangely dissociated from the scene she was watching, as though it were the cliff-hanger in a soap opera finale…but this was real. As was the metallic taste of fear in her mouth.

The silent war of attrition lasted a few seconds before the lesser man's eyes widened and he turned his head and slid the blade back into the concealed sheath on his robe.

He had lost face and he was not going to retire gracefully. He began to gesticulate angrily as he shouted, but Abby noticed that the few growls of agreement from the audience of watching men were subdued. Clearly in the 'lay it on the table and measure it' stakes he had lost out big time.

The tall horseman appeared oblivious to the growing tension as he addressed his soft comments to the man who had been in charge of the flesh auction.

Her would-be purchaser bent in to listen and threw up his hands, turning to his audience and inviting them to share his contempt. The response was a low growl.

For his part, the tall stranger seemed utterly

oblivious to the threat that lay heavy in the air as he held out a hand and slid a ring off one long, brown finger, dropping it into the palm of the waiting man's extended hand, then sliding a metal-banded watch from his wrist and adding it to the auctioneer's spoils.

The man produced a flashlight from his pocket and turned away, his shoulders hunched as he examined his haul. Without another word he nodded and called out something to another man, who came across holding a rolled-up sheet of paper. He unrolled it and laid it on top of a crate that was acting as a table.

Was it a bill of sale?

The idea filled her with a mixture of revulsion and disbelief. This could not be happening; it was too surreal.

Without even looking at her the horseman took her arm and tugged her with him to the makeshift table. He took the offered pen and wrote what she presumed was his name on it.

He then turned and held the pen out to Abby, who stared at it as if it were a striking snake before she shook her head and tucked her hand behind her back.

'What is it?'

The music being blasted from several of the trucks that had masked the noise of his arrival came to Zain's aid again, covering his murmured response.

'You can read the small print later,' he said, his words betraying an urgency suggesting the odds of them getting out of here diminished the longer they remained. 'If you ever want to see your home and family again sign it right now, you little fool.'

Her eyes fluttered wide as they flew to his face—she had not expected a reply to her question, let alone one in perfect English.

She took a deep breath then let it out slowly. Why was she even hesitating when the alternative was even more grim? Abby gave an imperceptible nod. The words on the paper blurred as she bent towards it and the pen that had been thrust into her hand trembled.

She would have dropped it but for the steadying grip of the long brown fingers that curved over her hand and guided it to the paper.

She looked from the big hand that curved her trembling fingers around the pen to her shaky signature appearing on the paper but felt no connection to it.

She stood there like a statue while the horseman physically took the pen from her fingers, conscious of a low buzz of argument just to her right that became loud and a lot angrier as the

horseman rolled up the paper and put it inside
a pocket hidden inside his robe.

The girl looked up at him with glazed green
eyes—shock, he diagnosed, stifling a stab of
sympathy. He pushed it away; empathy was not
going to get them out of here. Clear thinking
was. There was nothing like the danger of a
life and death situation to focus a man, Zain
thought with a smile. A bit of luck thrown in
would also help.

In the periphery of his vision he was aware
of the argument that was escalating, fast becoming a brawl…others were drifting towards
it and sides were being taken.

'Come on,' he said through clenched teeth.

As his fingers curved around her elbow he
could feel the tremors that were shaking her
body. He pushed away a fresh stab of sympathy. His priority right now was getting out of
this camp before someone recognised him and
realised that he was worth more money than
any girl, even one with flaming hair, curves
and legs… He cut short his inventory and lifted
his gaze from the shapely limbs in question.

'Can you walk?' There wasn't a trace of
sympathy in the question.

Ignoring the fact her knees were shaking,

the woman lifted her chin and responded to what he could admit had been a cold, vaguely accusing question.

'Of course I can walk.' She was unsteady but she fell into step beside him. It was clear that he was still a danger in her eyes but she clearly saw he represented her way out of this awful place.

'We don't have all day.' Behind his impassive expression he was impressed that she was still walking, and she wasn't having hysterics... This was going to be easier if she was not having hysterics.

'Keep up.'

Clearly unused to looking up at many people, the woman tilted her chin to lob a look of resentment at his patrician profile. 'I'm trying,' she muttered between clenched teeth.

'Then try harder before they realise they could attempt to retake you despite the bride price I paid.' His glance travelled from the top of her flaming head to her feet and all the lush curves in between before trailing to his own hand, which looked oddly bare without the ring he had worn since his eighteenth birthday. 'Or me,' he added softly.

Luckily, he was the spare and not the heir. Through the dark screen of his lashes he calculated how many people could get between them and the waiting horse. It was encouraging to see that most had moved to join in the fracas they were swiftly moving away from. Zain was content for the men to fight amongst themselves. It was the possibility of their stopping long enough to unite against a common foe—namely himself and the redhead—that bothered him.

None of the thoughts passing through his head showed in his body language, however, as he had learnt a long time ago that appearances *did* matter. It wasn't about a macho reluctance to show weakness; it was common sense. Weakness would always be exploited by enemies, and that went pretty much double when the enemies in question were carrying weapons.

A spasm of impatience flickered across his lean features as the girl slowed and came to a nervous halt when they got within a few feet of the stallion.

'He won't bite…unless you annoy him.'

Abby's experience of equines had until this point in her life been restricted to a donkey ride on the beach. Even at eleven, her long legs had almost touched the floor as she straddled the little donkey, who had plodded along and looked at her with sad eyes. This animal, with his stamping feet, looked about ten feet tall and his rolling eyes were not kind.

'I don't think he likes me.'

The mysterious stranger ignored the comment and vaulted into the saddle before reaching down and casually hauling her up before him.

Landing breathlessly, Abby clutched at the first thing that came to hand, which was the horseman, seizing on cloth. His body was hard as rock with zero excess flesh.

It wasn't until the horse had stopped dancing like a temperamental ballerina and she had not fallen off that the comment hit her. *Bride price…?*

'Can you do something with that hair? I can't see a damned thing…' Holding the reins in one hand, he pushed a skein of her copper hair away from his face and urged the horse into a canter. 'Yes, we just got married.'

She turned her head to stare in wide-eyed alarm as he urged all several hundred pounds of quivering, high-bred horse flesh underneath them into action, and the animal hit full gallop in seconds.

Her shriek was carried away by the warm

air that hit her face. Abby tightened her white-knuckled grip and closed her eyes, sending up a silent prayer…or maybe not so silent. She felt rather than heard his heartless laugh as the sting of sand hitting her face made her turn it protectively into his broad shoulder.

'Just hang on.'

She had no intention of letting go or, for that matter, opening her eyes again as her stomach lurched sickly. She couldn't see a thing anyway as they left the lights of the encampment behind. It was pitch-black. How on earth could he see where they were going?

Where *were* they going?

And were they really *married*?

The horse's thundering stride didn't falter. In fact, after a short time, the rhythm of its hoof beats seemed to have a *soothing* effect on her. Although perhaps that was too strong a word to describe the calm, almost hypnotic sensation allowing the rigidity of terror to slip from her body by degrees, allowing her to even lift her face from the man's shoulder.

'Are they following us?'

'Maybe. I only managed to disable half the engines before—' He cut off abruptly as he felt an echo of the swell of rage that had consumed him when he saw the guy raise his hand. 'Did they…hurt you?'

'Not in the way you mean.' She pressed a hand to her mouth to stifle a yawn. It wasn't fear that kept her eyes closed now but the fact that the mere effort of lifting her eyelids was a struggle.

But she had to try—there were questions she needed to ask. Not deep, meaningful stuff, just the basics, like who was he and where were they going?

'This is mad,' she said as another yawn escaped her. She felt weirdly numb and even her bitten arm seemed to have stopped hurting. Eyes closed, hurtling along like this felt strangely like flying, the hand that was looped casually around her ribs keeping her safe.

'No, it's physiology. Shock releases chemicals.'

And never underestimate the power of chemicals, he thought, the memory of the burst of raw rage that had hit him like a tsunami when he had seen the redhead paraded like a piece of meat for the benefit of the pack of rabid scum still fresh in his mind.

For a man who had always taken his ability to approach problems from the vantage point of cool detachment, the knowledge that his struggle to control the initial primal instinct, the rush of visceral hatred, to rush in without considering the consequences when it could have gone either way was disturbing.

'I'm not in shock,' she told him, a hint of challenge in her voice as she prised her eyelids apart and gave her head a tiny shake.

He flashed a look downwards at the woman who sat in front of him. The angle meant her face was hidden from him and he could only see the top of her glossy head and the angle of her jaw. It was a stubborn angle, but it had taken more than stubbornness to stand there and throw a punch. It was stupid, yes, but also just about the gutsiest thing he had ever seen.

'The danger is over and your adrenaline levels are dipping.'

Abby gave a tiny choking laugh, as if she thought the idea she was out of danger was funny.

'You've found something to laugh about in this situation?'

'I can have hysterics if you prefer,' she said with annoyance, a strange look coming over her face. Then, 'I feel sick,' she warned him suddenly.

'Don't be,' he said, knowing it was an unfeeling response but also knowing they couldn't stop now. It wasn't safe.

Luckily for them both her nausea passed, but the bone-deep exhaustion didn't as he felt her fight the losing battle to stay awake. At last she gave in and when her head next slumped against his chest it stayed there, her breathing deepening and her body relaxing into his.

Zain dragged her soft, limp body in closer, giving the powerful animal free rein, and found the quiet place in his head that had eluded him all day. It turned out that all it took was being fired at, giving away a priceless gem that had been in his family for generations, and having a beautiful, albeit filthy and bedraggled, woman snore softly in his arms. Just when he'd thought life was getting predictable.

His narrowed glance moved once more towards the east, where he could see a ribbon of distant lights that indicated they were being pursued, but they had had a head start and if he made a detour to the Qu'raing oasis their paths would not cross.

The danger was over…so why did he feel as if he was about to face another?

CHAPTER THREE

'TIME TO STRETCH your legs.'

Abby murmured sleepily and ignored the voice but couldn't ignore the creak of leather and the abrupt removal of the hard warmth she had been pressed against—as illusions of security went, this one was on an epic scale.

Abby fought her way through the layers of sleep and blinked… The ground was a long way off and the horse she sat astride was stamping and snorting restlessly.

She'd been asleep. How on *earth* had she actually slept?

She arched her back to stretch out the cricks in her spine and felt herself slip, so she grabbed the first thing that came to hand—a piece of horse mane—to regain her balance. Feeling slightly more secure, she risked letting go for a moment to brush away the hair that had fallen across her face, effectively blinding her.

She was half-inclined to pull the silky curtain back in place when her eyes connected with those of the tall man standing, arms folded across his chest, watching her.

Of their own volition, her eyes made the journey up from his dusty boots to the edges of the gold embroidery along the traditional gown he wore. Her throat drying as they reached his face, she lost interest in moving away. He was beautiful in a sharp-intake-of-breath, tummy-clenching way. The carved symmetry of his dark, dramatic features framed by the pale head-covering was riveting.

She quickly shook off her rapt expression, looking away and silently blaming her fascination with the carnal curve of this man's mouth on the situation… Everything that had happened felt more akin to an out-of-body experience than reality.

'I'd prefer not to stop,' she said.

'Is that a fact?'

His tone made her flush. 'I just meant…the thing is… I wasn't alone when they—' She stopped as, without warning, a wave of revulsion tightened like a fist in her stomach, an echo of the fear she had felt when she had been thrown in the truck. It took her a couple of swallows to regain enough composure to finish huskily, 'When they took me.'

He watched her thoughtfully as she fought for control.

'They, the rest of the group I was travelling with, are stranded—we *have* to…' She stopped, frustrated because he didn't seem to grasp the urgency.

'They are three grown men.'

Relief rushed through her; she'd asked her captors what had happened to the men left behind but the only response she'd had she hadn't been able to understand. 'You saw them?' she said eagerly.

He tipped his head in acknowledgement.

'They're not hurt? Did they get the car going?'

'They have shelter; they can survive a night in the desert.'

'You haven't reported their whereabouts to anyone?'

'Following you seemed a priority at the time.'

She bit her lip. 'And obviously I'm very grateful. I'm just worried about my friends.'

'One special friend perhaps?'

The insinuation made her flush. 'They are work colleagues. I'm a model. Now, if you don't mind, I would like to go and check, just to be sure.'

'Be my guest.'

* * *

He took a step back and spread an arm in a sweeping gesture towards the miles upon miles of undulating ochre sand. The first fingers of the rising sun had drawn a line of deep red along the horizon and he knew she was seeing a vast, terrifying emptiness, but Zain also knew that it teemed with life and all around them the nocturnal creatures that inhabited the vastness were hiding away from the oncoming day and the heat it brought.

'Which way do you suggest we go?'

She took refuge from frustration in a childish retort. 'So what you're telling me is to shut up and do as I'm told because you know best.'

Head tilted, he considered her comment. 'In the desert, I definitely know best,' he retorted calmly. 'You coming down?'

'Where are we?'

Not civilisation; the pale grey light of dawn revealed that much. There was something that looked like grass under their feet and a few scrubby trees to their left which blocked the view beyond. Behind them lay the seemingly endless miles of bare, bleak desert blushed pink by the dawn. She shivered again.

* * *

He had never seen skin so smooth, features so crystal-clear… He brought his list of her attributes to an abrupt halt. Her beauty had made her a victim today, but it was inevitable that there had been many occasions when it had played to her advantage, when men had made fools of themselves over her.

Zain dragged his eyes, which were inclined to linger on the long length of her slim, shapely legs, upwards. The twist of his lips held self-mockery as he observed, 'It's a bit late in the day for caution, don't you think?' His heart might be in cold storage but it seemed his libido was still active and functioning.

Maybe that was the way forward?

Not here, not now and *definitely* not with a woman who probably didn't even realise how vulnerable she was. But empty sex, while not exactly an original way to move on, was a tried and tested method and appealed to him a hell of a lot more than drowning in self-pity or becoming celibate.

Sex was healthy if you kept it free of emotions. And he had learnt to control his years ago…mostly… Unbidden, the moment he had got his first glimpse of the kidnapped woman flashed into his mind.

When he set out to find her he'd had no mental image in his head of the woman he was seeking—she hadn't actually been a person for him. Regardless, nothing he could imagine would have come close to the reality.

He hadn't needed the cacophony of competing music blaring from the trucks to cover his entrance into the ramshackle encampment. All attention had been fixed on her. In a heartbeat the electric air of anticipation in the place had been explained. It had taken Zain a moment to absorb every detail of her lithe, lush body, the impossibly long legs, the sinuous curves, the pale skin and tangled skein of flaming auburn hair. There was nothing plastic or air-brushed about her—just a warm, luscious, desirable woman.

It wasn't difficult to imagine her on a billboard selling anything and maybe causing a few accidents. She was the sort of woman to make a man forget about his troubles. Not that he was that man but, even so, the last few miles with her soft body pressed against his had made for an interesting journey—just him, the sleeping girl and his testosterone. There was a simplicity to it that, after a day of his calculating his every expression and verbal intonation, had been a strange sort of relief.

* * *

It took a couple of seconds for Abby's exhausted, stress-racked brain to pick its way through the man's critical comment.

'You think it was *my* fault I got kidnapped? I *asked* for it maybe…? You know, one of the things I despise most is victim-blaming…not that I am—a victim, I mean—but…oh, hell!' She threw up her hands, immediately losing her balance and a couple of wild, flailing moments later falling straight into his open arms.

The impact of hitting a chest that was as hard as steel expelled a soft whoosh of air from her lungs as the arm banding her ribs loosened enough to let her slide slowly all the way to the floor. It was obvious before she made land fall that the rest of him was equally hard—the man was built of solid muscle—and falling had felt less alarming than the head-spinning, stomach-fluttering sensation that made her world spin. The sensation was so strong it was a breathless moment before she managed to get her erratic breathing under control enough to protest.

'Let me g…go!'

He did, with a care that bordered, unexpectedly, on tenderness. 'I'm not the one doing the holding,' he pointed out, angling a quizzical look at her fingers still clutching the sleeves of his robe.

Before she could react to the taunting reminder, the blades of his dark brows drew into an interrogative straight line above his spectacular, dazzling blue eyes. 'What's *that*?'

She lifted a hand to the puffy, swollen area on her arm where his accusatory glance rested. 'A bite, I suppose.'

He laid one hand on her forehead, caught her wrist with the other and extended her arm, bending in closer to inspect the area.

'Do you mind? That hurts!' she protested, turning her head away and tugging on her arm; after what had happened it seemed bizarre that he had fixated on this minor problem.

'So you dress like you're off to play a game of beach volleyball, and for good measure don't use mosquito repellent. Do you know how dangerous this desert is?'

Fighting the urge to pull at the hem of her shorts to cover herself from his contemptuous gaze, she lifted her chin a defiant notch and cut across him.

'It was a photo shoot. I don't choose what I wear, and I did use repellent.' It had been in the sunscreen that she had virtually bathed in. 'If it's all the same to you, I'd prefer to go straight back to my hotel,' she announced.

He looked startled, then, after a short, stunned-seeming silence, gave a laugh. 'I am not a taxi service.'

The amused hauteur in his response made her feel marginally less awful about coming across like some sort of snooty tourist, but she could see he had a point.

Her descent from snooty was rapid and clearly not at all what he'd expected. 'Of course not. Sorry. And I suppose it's a bit late but I'm tremendously… Thank you,' she said, her gratitude as genuine as her hope he really was one of the good guys. She felt the ball of fear in her stomach tightening and refused to acknowledge it.

The groove between his brows deepened. Her rescuer hadn't expected the back-down and it threw him, as did the obvious genuineness of it. 'I don't require your thanks.'

The lingering shock in her system made her response teary. 'Tough, I'm grateful.'

'What were you doing all the way out there alone anyway?' His question had an unexpected throaty quality.

Abby took a breath, feeling tears press against her eyelids, and tried to flatten out her emotional response. Facts, she could do facts.

'We were meant to be much closer to the city, but nobody had factored in the wedding. Did you know? Sorry, it doesn't matter.' All her efforts focused on not sounding weepy, she avoided his eyes. That bright, glittering stare made it hard for her to concentrate. 'But it did complicate things—there was a no-fly zone, diversions and a lot of restrictions.' They had sat in an airport lounge drinking coffee while emails between the firm paying for the jaunt and the director decided their fate. 'I even wondered at first when I was…' Catching herself up short, she gave a self-conscious little nod. She swallowed, her hand pressed to her throat as she relived those awful moments when the men had grabbed her. 'I wondered, actually *hoped* it was a set-up for publicity…' She swallowed again and rubbed her hands over her forearms, remembering the sensations of total, overwhelming helplessness. 'I feel grubby.' She wasn't talking just about the sand clinging to her skin and hair or the assorted smears of dirt on her inadequate clothing.

'Then come.' He tipped his head towards the trees. 'Bathe.'

She blinked at the unexpected response.

'A horse needs water.' He took hold of the horse's reins and approached the scrubby undergrowth.

The incline had not been apparent from where they had stood but it explained why she hadn't been able to see the taller trees or the palms. An oasis meant water and soon they reached it, a bubbling trickle that rose up from the ground and ran in a thin silver ribbon through the trees. Neither horse nor rider paused; instead they carried on, the reason becoming clear a few moments later when the stream fed into a pool of turquoise water framed by palms.

Her exposure to life's ugliness had given her a new appreciation of life's beauty, and emotion deepened her voice as she stared at the shimmering, postcard-perfect image and gasped. 'It's beautiful!'

The stranger watched her battle to subdue the tears, blinking and sniffing but stubbornly determined not to add any new tear tracks to her face as she pressed a hand to her soft, trembling lips. Standing there, bedraggled, her face filthy and scratched, she knew she looked ridiculously fragile. Stubborn pride was the only thing holding her up.

'We need to do something about your arm.'

The first hint of gentleness in his voice released the floodgates and the tears began to overflow, sliding down her cheeks as first one sob escaped her lips then another. They just kept coming…deep, subterranean sobs that shook her entire body.

Without thinking, Zain reacted to her distress. He moved in closer, took her by the arms and stood there, bodies close but not touching, his chin on her head while she wailed like a banshee. One look at her tear-filled eyes and the fear warring with pride there had touched him in a corner of his heart he hadn't known existed.

The sobs and tremors shaking her body subsided and finally she pulled away, looking embarrassed rather than grateful.

'I must look terrible,' she sniffed, not quite meeting his eyes.

'Yes,' he agreed, too distracted by the scene playing in his head to display any tact.

She was under him, her warmth pushing up into him, her body arching as he slid deep inside her.

He'd known her barely a few hours and already it was becoming a recurrent theme that his imagination was intermittently adding erotic details to. More a man for action, Zain had never thought fantasies were any substitute for reality. What he hadn't realised until this moment was just how frustrating they were!

His distracted response made her forget her determination not to look at him. As she did, the startled indignation on her face melted into amusement and she broke the silence with a gurgle of laughter. 'Well, at least I know you're honest now. Which means… I'm safe.' She paused, as if giving it time to sink in. 'I didn't think that…'

She had a very expressive face and he could virtually see the nightmare scenes playing through her head.

'Then don't think,' he recommended, guilt at his lustful thoughts making him sound abrupt. She had just escaped hell and his empathy amounted to fixating on the lush promise of her incredible mouth—and for that matter the lush promise of the rest of her. Hell, but you're a sensitive guy, he told himself sardonically.

'I'm just relieved that I'm safe.' And with relief came a deep exhaustion and she made no protest when he urged her down onto the grass beside the pool.

Leaving her there, Zain walked over to where the stallion was grazing and pulled out a thermos that was tucked into one of the saddlebags. Dropping down into a squat beside her, he unscrewed the top and handed it to her.

She drank greedily, wiping her lips when she'd finished then handing it back.

He couldn't keep calling her 'the redhead' and he'd forgotten what the men had called her. 'Do you have a name?'

'Abby. And you are?'

'Zain.'

'Let me see your arm, Abby.'

He inspected it gently before nodding, then looking around. 'Stay put.'

Abby doubted of she could have moved even if she'd wanted to. Still, she followed him with her eyes—he was easy to watch and the way he moved…the combination of power, grace and perfect co-ordination…her stomach gave a lazy flip before she snatched her glance guiltily away.

There was no harm looking, was there?

Actually, if she *hadn't* been looking she really would need the medical attention as badly as he seemed to think she did. If she met a woman who could pronounce herself indifferent to what this man oozed she would know she was in the presence of a liar!

'This might sting.'

Might...? She bit her lower lip to stop herself crying out when he poured water over the bite. 'Are those leaves?' she asked, watching doubtfully as he laid something over the red, swollen area.

'Neem leaves… Hold it there.'

This time he walked down to the water. He unfastened the gold rope that held his headdress in place before pulling the white cloth of his head-covering free.

Abby felt a little stab of shock; she had just assumed that his hair would be long, in keeping with the whole Bedouin thing…but it was short, very dark, but for a fairer streak near the hairline at the front.

Her fascination increased as she watched him run his hand across the short strands, making them stand on end in sexy tufts before he squatted down, splashed water on his face and head, and pulled a knife from a fold in his gown.

He turned his head and she looked away quickly, guilty that she'd been caught staring like a child with her nose pressed to the window of a sweet shop, except the thoughts that went through her head when she looked at him were not innocent or childlike.

'What is neem?' she asked, watching as he split the white fabric with the knife, tearing it into several strips.

Still in the crouching position, he leaned back on his heels and pointed upwards. 'A tree—that one there and those over there.'

She shaded her eyes and looked up into the canopy of the tree he indicated.

'People have been using neem medicinally for centuries for any number of conditions; it's said to have antiseptic properties, so here's hoping.'

'That it's not an old wives' tale?'

'A lot of scientific research suggests otherwise. Pharmaceutical firms are taking an interest; Aarifa has developed a project farming the trees. They grow fast, literally anywhere, in any soil, and a deep, extensive root system means they can survive drought.'

She looked more impressed than the old guard—all men—had been when he'd explained the same thing to them. They'd all held positions of power in Aarifa for a generation and were negative about any idea that originated in his office, but Zain believed in it and had pushed on regardless. Ultimately, he'd been proven right.

The project he'd proposed had been a commercial success, bringing investment from foreign companies, creating much needed jobs and inspiring home-grown entrepreneurial talent in the shape of a couple who had developed a cosmetics line using the plant.

Abby, holding her hair back from her face, watched him take a leaf and crush it between his long fingers before pressing it into a piece of wet fabric. He did it with the same precision that characterised everything he did.

'You sound like a teacher.'

His eyes lifted momentarily from his task before he continued. 'I'm not.'

He could tell she was curious but her reluctance to reveal her interest stopped her from bombarding him with questions.

'A bit makeshift—it needs grinding to make a proper poultice—but it's better than nothing.'

'How do you know about this stuff…do you live in the desert?' she probed casually and again he framed a reply that told her nothing.

'Life is simpler in the desert.'

And that had a certain appeal, but time was the issue. His yearly month-long sabbatical, when he returned to his roots and his paternal grandmother's family, who still lived a traditional tribal Bedouin existence, had this year become a begrudging two weeks… How long before it was just a memory?

'You can let go now.'

He took the leaf that adhered to her skin and replaced it with the wet fabric wad covered with the ground leaves of the tree, deftly wrapping another one of the fabric strips around to hold it in place.

He arched a brow. 'Not too tight?'

She shook her head, lowering her gaze from his.

'My shoe is though,' she said, waggling her right foot at him. 'One foot is half a size bigger than the other.' He looked at her as though she were mad—she probably was.

'You need to drink some more water.'

Abby clenched her teeth at his order.

'Thanks.' She got the water bottle as far as her lips before something distracted her. A memory, perhaps.

Zain watched her eyes glaze as she stared, unfocused, into the distance. He was ready to catch the bottle when it slipped from her fingers.

The cynic in him wanted to believe her vulnerability was feigned as she blinked up at him like a baby owl, but he knew it wasn't.

'An imagination can be a curse.' His terse delivery hid the reluctant sympathy he felt.

Abby nodded and looked away, patting the damp spot where water had spilled, soaking a patch of her top before pooling in her cleavage. The action drew Zain's gaze and kick-started his own distracting imagination.

A curse, maybe. Painful, definitely.

He breathed his way through a bolt of mind-numbing molten lust—not so easy when in his head his hands were weighing those tight, high breasts and he was bending his head to taste the berry sweetness of the nipples.

'Your bite is infected...'

CHAPTER FOUR

SHE GLANCED AT his face, wondering what she had said to make him sound annoyed…or *more* annoyed.

'You should get it checked out when you get back to civilisation. You need a course of antibiotics asap.' He rose smoothly from his crouched position and stood over her, holding out a hand.

Abby took it. Standing beside him, she was again very conscious of his physical presence. She was used to looking down on men, or at least to looking most in the eye, and not so long ago had gone through life hunching her shoulders, embarrassed by her height and envying petite women.

'How long will it take to get back?' she asked, rubbing her hand against her thigh. The weird tingling impression remained.

'Half an hour or so, now that he's rested,'

Zain estimated. The stallion, as though sensing he was the subject of conversation, wandered over and nudged his master's arm, demanding attention.

So, back to normal life… She frowned, wondering why she didn't feel happier at the prospect. I'm lucky, she reminded herself; her life was something that many would have aspired to and it had fallen into her lap. More importantly, it was a means to an end, a way to give her grandparents back the life that had been stolen from them.

'Were you serious about…? Are we really… married?'

She had hoped he'd laugh, because it was infinitely preferable to be mocked than married to a total stranger.

'Don't worry, I'll sort it out.'

The acknowledgement that there was something to *sort out* tightened the tension curling in the pit of her stomach. 'So, what, you just wave your magic wand and snap your fingers? Or do you have your own legal team on standby?'

'I'll sort it,' he repeated calmly.

She couldn't hide her scepticism but clung to the hope it would turn out there was nothing to *sort*. 'I assume I should report what's happened to someone.' The thought of explaining to a foreign and not necessarily sympathetic police force what had happened was pretty daunting.

'I'll drop you off at the British Embassy. They'll sort things out for you.'

'Thank you.' She extended a hand to shake his then was struck by the sheer ludicrousness of the formality and leaned in, the leaning co-inciding with the exact moment the restless horse chose to butt her bottom quite firmly with his nose, literally pushing her into his master.

Zain's arms opened to stop her falling—strangely the sensation in her head was also exactly like falling as she looked up into his lean, darkly beautiful face. Safe in his em-brace, she wriggled her elbows, trying to free herself from the emotions the feelings of his arms around her unleashed. Her arms were squashed between their bodies but the urgency faded as her eyes drifted across the marvellous angles and planes of his face.

'I...' Her voice faded away as she felt a hard shudder run through his body and excitement sparked, kicking up the volume of her heart-beat. She could hear common sense issuing an irritating prissy whisper at the back of her mind and ignored it. Life was short—a fact that had been driven home today—and if you didn't take a chance, what was the point?

She couldn't take her eyes off the nerve she could see beating through the stubble on his lean cheek.

She expelled her breath on a long, gusty sigh. 'I really...'

Zain swallowed; in his head his fingernails were hanging on to the last shreds of his vanishing self-control. He felt like a man walking a tightrope—he wanted to grab on to all that lovely softness and not let go. Her cushiony lips looked so soft and inviting...would they taste as good as they looked?

She slid her hands up from between their bodies, her fingertips shaking as she touched his face, her expression rapt as she trailed them down his stubble-dusted cheeks.

Every cell in his body froze. Digging into reserves of control he didn't know he possessed, he took hold of her wrists and leaned back.

Zain had never had anything but contempt for men who took advantage of women. The boss who misused a position of power, the guy in the bar who honed in on the woman who couldn't walk straight, the best 'friend' who moved in to offer comfort after a tough divorce. They were *weak* men who took advantage, men like his brother, who would and had shown contempt for anything resembling scruples.

The idea of being the man his brother was filled Zain with utter blood-chilling horror.

But God, he was tempted.

'Abby.'

'I really want to say thank you.' She raised herself on tiptoe and closed her eyes, tilting her face up to his in silent invitation.

His head lowered and for a split second their glances connected and the deep, desperate need he felt was reflected in the drowning green of her eyes. Abby gave a tiny sigh as his mouth covered hers and his eyes squeezed closed as he surrendered himself totally to the sensation of the slow, sensuous brush of her lips.

This was insanity but it was a beautiful insanity. It made no sense but it didn't matter… it was not about logic, just need. A need she had never felt before, a need a million miles from the feelings Gregory's awkward kisses had summoned.

The sound of the groan that vibrated in his powerful chest escalated the dizzying excitement swirling through her veins. And when he dragged her in tight, sealing their bodies together and flaunting the hardness of his erection against her belly, Abby felt a primitive thrill sweep through her as she kissed him back.

And then, as quickly as it had begun, it was over. He had physically picked her up and set her a few feet away from him.

She blinked like someone coming up for air and then the realisation hit home and a moment later scalding humiliation.

'Sorry.'

What for? she thought. *Not fancying me?*

'I know it's not me...it's you.' Papering over her humiliation with pride, she lifted her chin. At least now she had that ability to take control of an awkward situation, unlike in her teens, when her much-anticipated date with one of the cool boys was revealed as a joke... *Like kissing a wet fish!* he'd told his friends at school. 'I never thought otherwise,' she lied.

'You need medical attention, not—'

'A roll in the hay...' she inserted, having learnt from bitter experience that it was always better to mock yourself before your detractors got the chance. 'You are *totally* right,' she agreed, thinking, The only medical attention I need involves a shrink's couch!

What the hell was she doing? She'd never acted like this in her life… The memory of his hands and mouth on her only moments ago made her want to hide from embarrassment, a feeling she remembered from her school days when she had been isolated, become a target for the cool girls and sniggered at by their boyfriends because she was too tall and thin and that swot who put her hand up in class. The situation had culminated in the fake date that had made her retreat even farther into her shell—at least she had got incredible grades.

It was hard to find an equivalent bright side to this situation.

'I'm ready when you are…oh, and I hope you're keeping a tab of how much I owe you for your time and…' She stopped, biting down on her inside lips as her eyes fell from his— what was the going rate for saving someone's life?

Zain shrugged off the insult. If he'd taken offence it would have been easier but his understanding expression made her feel even more of a total idiot!

'How about we call it…?' An expression she couldn't put a name to flickered across his face before he produced one of his inimical shrugs. 'Let's just call it good timing.'

He could call it anything he liked. She still didn't have a clue what he really meant.

'Fine.'

It was hard to project 'distant and aloof' when you were sitting in front of someone on a horse going very fast, so Abby was deeply relieved when the walled city with its iconic towers and minarets came into view.

It was bizarre but after everything that had happened to her it was the humiliation of throwing herself at him like some sort of sex-starved groupie that was eating away at her.

She was mad at herself, mad for setting herself up for the knock-back and for caring about it, and mad at him. Especially mad at him!

It wasn't until the first security checkpoint, some way outside the city limits, came into view that it occurred to her that they might have some difficulty re-entering the city.

Getting out had been complicated enough and then they had had a stack of stamped and signed documents. Now she didn't even have her passport and the man with her looked exactly the sort of dangerous character that would ring alarm bells.

Maybe he was thinking the same because he

brought the horse to a halt before they reached the actual checkpoint, dismounting and telling her to do the same.

She ignored the hand he extended and, though her solo dismount almost ended in disaster, she hadn't accepted his help, which at that moment was all that mattered, a childish display of defiance but the only defence she had against her humiliation.

'Have you got the right permits? Shall I talk to them?'

'Stay here.'

It wasn't clear if he was talking to her or the horse but he didn't look back, so presumably it never crossed his mind that either of them would disobey his command.

She watched as he walked straight up to the men in uniform and hoped he wasn't going to take the same high-handed attitude with them.

The conversation only lasted a few minutes and the guards' guns had stayed across their shoulders. That had to be a good sign, didn't it?

Her anxiety climbed as the minutes ticked by. Were they grilling him? When he turned and began to walk back towards her she felt a wave of relief that vanished when one of the guards followed him, jogging to catch up with the tall, dominant figure. A telltale flame of desire that Abby wanted badly to deny ignited low down in her belly as she watched him.

It took for ever for them to reach her and the expression on his arrestingly beautiful face gave her no clues as to how the discussion had gone, but no one was waving any guns, which was a step in the right direction.

The guard tipped his head to Abby and said something that didn't sound aggressive—in fact it sounded almost deferential.

'He said he is sorry about your experiences and hopes that it has not given you a bad impression of our country.'

Abby smiled and nodded at the man. 'Did he really say that?'

'Word for word,' Zain responded but the look in his eyes suggested he had missed a few things out in his translation.

'So, what happens now?'

As if in response to her question a jeep drove towards them stopping only a few feet away. A driver wearing a military uniform got out and walked towards them and for a split second she thought his extended hand held a weapon or at least a set of handcuffs, but then she saw that the metal the sun had glinted off was a bunch of keys attached to a key ring.

Zain held out his hand for the keys, delivered some sort of instructions to the driver and then sent him on his way.

Abby hadn't understood a word of the one-sided conversation and felt her confusion grow as she watched the man lead the stallion away.

'You can't let them take your horse,' she protested.

'I thought you did not like horses.'

'That's not the point—you can't trade an animal for a…a…'

'The horse doesn't have air-conditioning. Relax, I am joking.'

'Joking?'

'I have not exchanged my horse.' His lips twitched at some sort of inside joke she wasn't privy to. 'They are merely going to look after him for me.'

'And let you use this in the meantime?' She continued to regard him with extreme scepticism. 'Did you bribe them or something?' she called out as he got into the driving seat.

Zain leant out of the window. 'I simply explained the situation. Now get in.'

Abby did so, not that she was in any way convinced by his story. She knew she was missing something, but what? He started the engine almost before she had closed the door.

'You're not telling me everything. Have you got connections or something?'

'I have an honest face and they have my horse as hostage. It was a simple negotiation.'

It sounded plausible but the conviction she was missing something persisted.

Clearly he knew the city well, as he drove quickly and efficiently, diverting on numerous occasions down side streets when they encountered traffic jams or when some of the parties that still seemed to be going on had blocked entire roads.

The party atmosphere seemed to have infected the policemen on duty as well because they were waved through the numerous security checkpoints without being stopped once. It couldn't have gone smoother if they'd been part of the wedding party.

'This is it.'

He pulled the jeep up outside a building with wrought-iron railings, the only thing differentiating it from the other buildings lining both sides of the affluent-looking but narrow street the small, discreet sign above the door.

She turned in her seat. 'I don't know your name, and you've... People say the words "you've saved my life" all the time.' She done it herself when someone handed her a coffee she needed particularly badly. 'But you *really* have. You're a genuine hero.' For the first time, she saw him look acutely uncomfortable. 'And just when I thought you didn't have a weak spot,' she murmured, half to herself.

'Right place, right time...that's all.'

She shook her head and reached for the door handle, inadvertently knocking her injured arm. She clenched her teeth as fighting the pain was a lot easier than fighting the throb of awareness she felt every time she looked at this man. It was so strange because she didn't normally react this way to men—she never had, certainly not with Gregory, whose appeal had been the fact he seemed safe...turned out, of course, he was anything but!

Zain was opening the passenger door before she had even registered he was getting out. While Abby nursed her throbbing arm against her chest he took her other and helped her out. 'Be careful and get that arm checked out straight away.'

'I will,' she promised, looking at him and feeling the traitorous trickle of heat between her legs. Why did she react to him this way, a way she had never reacted to a man before? 'It's actually feeling better, I think.'

She thought about shaking his hand but remembered how that had turned out the last time and thought better of it, instead tipping her head solemnly in thanks.

He nodded, turned and strode back to the car. She had the craziest impulse to run after him before he vanished from her life, but common sense prevailed before she had made a fool of herself for a second time—he never had been part of her life so there was no reason to change that now.

Abby walked to the embassy door, glad he couldn't see the tears that filled her eyes, unaware that someone else could.

In the basement of the British Embassy a man sitting beside several monitors turned and called out to his colleague, who was dozing in a chair.

'Call Mr Jones; I think he'll want to see this.' He scrolled the image back several frames and froze the streamed recording, zooming in on the face of the man that many privately called the man who should be the next sheikh.

Pity Zain Al Seif was only second in line.

CHAPTER FIVE

Ten months later

EVEN IN AN area where conspicuous wealth and status symbols were the norm, the low-slung silver designer car sitting glinting in the afternoon attracted attention and covetous stares, but not as much attention or as many stares as the man who walked along the tree-lined boulevard towards it. Even had he been dressed in charity-shop rejects, the man would have stopped traffic. He had an almost tangible aura, authority mingled with masculinity in its most raw form.

Zain was oblivious to the swivelled heads and raised designer shades as his attention was focused not on the car, but on its owner.

He was a few feet away when the crowd of giggling young women that had surrounded the man when he got out of his car parted to reveal someone he didn't immediately recognise. When recognition did strike, his eyes widened behind the darkened lenses of his shades and he made a rapid mental calculation. In the—what?—six weeks since he'd last seen his brother, Khalid, whose dissipated lifestyle, lack of self-control and love of excess had made him pile on the pounds and look older than his thirty-two years, had lost a good twenty pounds.

Perhaps it was the speed of the dramatic weight loss that was responsible for the drawn look on his brother's face, and Zain's jaw tightened as Khalid curved his hand around the bottom of one of the giggling women. The waistline might have improved but clearly his brother's morals had not, as, for better or most probably for worse, his brother was married.

So are you. Zain's lips twisted into an ironic half-smile as he recognised the element of hypocrisy in his disapproval—or, at least, it would have been hypocrisy had his marriage existed anywhere but on a piece of paper signed under a desert sky.

There was an added irony to the situation in that he was the one brother who hadn't actually cheated.

Of course, his fidelity was of the purely accidental variety and nothing to do with respecting his marriage vows or the lingering

memory of the redhead he had married—
that would have been insane. Instead his celi-
bacy had been the consequence of a non-stop
work schedule so intense that he hadn't yet got
around to doing something about the marriage
certificate still sitting in his safe.

He had considered the simpler option of
burning the offending sheet of paper but after
a period of reflection he had opted to retain the
document rather than destroy it. Less 'doing the
right thing' and more the conviction that history
was littered with men brought down not by the
mistakes they made but the denial of their mistakes—the cover-ups and the lies that turned a
minor blip into an earthquake of scandal.

Zain had never doubted there *would* be a
scandal. The only question was the degree of
damage caused by a story, so in the interests of
damage limitation it had made sense to find out
as much as he could about Miss Abigail Foster.

But so far there had been no approach from
her agents, no tabloid headlines, no talk of
book deals, no rumours circulating at all that
he had been made aware of. The only reference
to a rescue had been at a British Embassy dinner by one of the anonymous suits, who, letting him know *he* knew, had assured Zain of
his *complete discretion*.

The man had also made a suggestion that might explain why there had been no attempt to cash in on the story.

'I'm not sure that Miss Foster, a rather naïve young lady, I think, actually knew who you were.'

The image that floated into his head slowed his stride as he recalled the details of that perfect oval face, which was dominated by extraordinary eyes framed by dark lashes the same sooty black as the sweeping brows.

'Zain, glad you could make it.' Pushing away the distracting image, but not before his body had hardened in reaction, Zain held his brother's eyes as Khalid slid an arm around the waist of the nearest blonde and, leaning in close, said something that made her giggle.

It took effort but Zain didn't deliver the reaction the provocative action had been designed to shake loose and his facial expression stayed locked in neutral, the contempt in his eyes concealed by the mirrored lenses of his designer shades.

After a moment, Khalid let the girl go, his expression petulant as he nodded to one of the minders standing a few feet away, the man quickly reacting and ushering the fawning crowd away.

Khalid did not speak until the sound of their high heels had vanished.

He stood to one side and pulled open one of the doors, inviting his brother with a nod to look inside the interior of the expensive plaything. 'So, what do you think? They have only made five of these beauties…'

'I think that the people affected by the cuts to the health budget might question your priorities.'

Khalid's laughter was not a pleasant sound and neither was the hacking cough that followed it.

As the paroxysm of coughs continued Zain's brow creased in a frown of reluctant concern, though his eyes remained wary as he framed his brusque question. 'Are you all right?'

A white linen handkerchief pressed to his mouth, Khalid straightened up, his eyes above the white filled with glittering black enmity that was in stark contrast to his words as he took away the handkerchief and made his response without answering his brother's question. 'So, you think the health cuts are a bad idea?'

Zain lifted one darkly defined brow. 'And I'm meant to believe that you are actually interested in what I think?'

The handkerchief spoilt the line of his tailored trousers as Khalid shoved it back into his pocket and pulled the passenger door wide. 'We don't have to be enemies, do we?' His sigh was deep and his tone wistful.

An olive-branch moment. Logic and experience should have made Zain walk away, but he didn't. Instead he called himself a fool and stood there thinking optimistically that maybe it was true what they said about blood being thicker than water. Either that or he was certifiable.

Zain dragged a hand across his dark hair, the action weary. 'I'm not your enemy, Khalid.' Something flashed in his brother's eyes but it vanished too quickly for Zain to tell if it was anything more than a trick of the light.

'I've always been jealous of you, you know. Your friends, your—'

'You have friends.'

Khalid gave a hard laugh. 'I buy people... that doesn't make them my friends.'

Zain had never imagined his brother capable of such insight, let alone the courage to admit it aloud.

'Come, let's not argue. Take a drive with me.' Khalid pulled the door wider. 'I haven't put her through her paces yet.'

After a pause, Zain got in.

'All buckled up?' Khalid asked, glancing at his brother. 'You can't be too careful. I thought we'd take the scenic route.'

Zain glanced at the speedometer as they hit the first bend. His brows lifted at the number on the dial, but he didn't feel nervous—his half-brother was bad at many things but driving wasn't one of them.

By the time they hit the third bend on a road famous for its hairpin turns and the crashes they had caused, a layer of tension had descended onto his shoulders.

'Do you want me to slow down, little brother?' Khalid mocked as he overtook a lorry on a bend, pulling in just in time to avoid a car coming in the opposite direction.

'Are you high?' Zain asked.

'High on life…high on…actually I probably am, though the drugs don't really work the same now. You see, little brother, I'm dying. I have lung cancer and it's already spread. I'm terminal.'

'Medical—'

'Advances are made every day. I know. But I also know they won't work for me.' The low purr of the car became a growl as he floored it once more around the next bend.

'It's not too late for us to—'

'Bury the hatchet? How heroically noble and so very *Zain*...' he spat. 'But it's too late for that. Don't look sad, brother, we all die. But knowing the when and the how...that changes things, gives you back the power. Yes,' he said, watching with a smile as Zain's hand moved to the door handle. 'It's locked, but going at this speed you'd die even if you could open it.

'You know, the worst thing about learning I was going to die was knowing that *you'd* be there after me, taking my place on the throne... in my wife's bed...but now it's fine because I've realised that death is actually a gift. Because I can take you with me.'

Zain lunged to take the wheel but his brother kept the car on its trajectory, a trajectory that would send it sailing off the cliff and into space. Zain transferred his attentions to the door, slamming and kicking to gain his freedom.

'Relax and enjoy it, little brother. I intend to.' Khalid's laugh turned into a cry of rage as the door finally gave and Zain threw himself through it.

Wide, cool corridors radiated out from the octagonal central atrium, where light from the glass dome sparked rainbow reflections off the water cascading from the fountain into a mosaic-lined pool.

It felt more like a five-star hotel than any hospital Abby had ever experienced, certainly nothing like the ones she remembered from her childhood. She'd been six when she had first arrived at one in the back of an ambulance. She remembered the rush of cold December air that brushed over her before the trolley she had lain on was pushed through a wide set of double doors and whisked along what had seemed a never-ending corridor. The lights shining down from the ceiling had made her head ache.

There was a gap in her recollections between that point and later when she'd found herself sitting in a hard-backed chair, her feet not touching the floor as she swung them. She had been counting in her head the trail of bright red splodges on the tiled floor that stopped at the curtain that hid from view the people who were making the loud noises, the people who were trying to save her parents.

They'd tried for a long time. Abby had climbed out of the chair and wandered off long before they'd admitted defeat. Her gran told the story of how she'd been found later, thumb in mouth, asleep on the floor of a sluice room.

'Sorry to keep you waiting.'

Abby dropped the hand she'd raised to shade her eyes from the rainbow colours dancing on the water and turned, the motion displacing the silk scarf that her British escort had handed her before they stepped out of the car... *Not essential but a nice gesture*, he'd said.

She knew the green filaments in the scarf emphasised the deep emerald of her eyes and she adjusted it again over the burnished waves of her hair, which seemed determined not to be covered.

'Will we be able to fly back tonight, Mr Jones?

'We all want this situation to be resolved as swiftly as possible,' came the frustratingly vague response.

His voice, like everything else about the man, was nondescript and unmemorable. Abby had only encountered him once before and if it had not been for the extraordinary circumstances under which they'd met, she doubted she ever would have remembered him. And circumstances didn't get much more extraordinary than the ones that had preceded her arrival at the British Embassy in the Aarifan capital city ten months ago.

She'd told her story to at least half a dozen people before Mr Jones appeared, and over another cup of tea she had related her tale yet again. He had listened, then pressed her on a few specific points. Had she actually read the document she'd signed? Had the man who'd come to her rescue given his name?

His gentle persistence had sent alarm bells ringing in her head.

'I'm not actually married though, right? It wasn't real…?'

He'd been very soothing on that point and told her *absolutely not*. He'd then advised her to forget what had happened and to go home and get on with her life.

So Abby had. Well, she had got on with her life. Forgetting was another thing. Her memories had taken on a surreal dream-like quality, the man who rescued her the stuff fantasies were made of.

Fantasies had no place in Abby's life though; she was too busy for that nonsense. Though the tall fantasy figure did insert himself into her dreams, and even then she frequently didn't recall the details of the dreams he'd invaded but she'd know he'd been there by the heavy, nameless ache in the pit of her stomach that lingered when she awoke…*too soon*, it always felt.

Mr Jones had been the last person she had expected to see waiting outside her flat door when she arrived home yesterday afternoon after a particularly depressing appointment with the agents selling her grandparents' old home.

The timing couldn't have been worse. She had just about put together enough money for the deposit and she had a mortgage in place… She'd assumed all she'd have to do was sign on the dotted line. The man had not laughed outright in her face, but he had come close.

'I'm afraid, Miss Foster, that the housing market has been buoyant since your grandparents sold. The present vendors are asking—' He scrolled down the page on his tablet and read out a number so crazy that initially Abby thought he was joking. Sadly, he wasn't.

Mr Jones also hadn't been joking when, flanked by two men in Arab robes, he explained that it turned out she *was* married after all and her 'husband' was the younger son of the Sheikh Aban Al Seif, the ruler of Aarifa.

And all before she'd even got through the door!

Abby was still assimilating this news when, seated on her sofa that was badly in need of reupholstering, Mr Jones worked his way up to his next big reveal, fortifying himself first with a Rich Tea biscuit.

'There is no need to be upset, Miss Foster; the mistake was little more than an unfortunate clerical error.'

'So, can I sign something?' she asked.

'Ah, well, there is the rub. Normally I would be able to say yes but, well, the accident means that the doctors are unlikely to agree to Zain Al Seif travelling for some weeks, and the legal process means that your signatures both need to be witnessed by...'

One word in the bland, meandering explanation had leapt out at Abby as an image flashed into her head so real that, for a moment, Zain seemed to be standing there, physically imposing, the same way he'd looked when she had first seen him striding into the encampment—a beautiful man exuding an arrogance and command that was mesmerising. 'What do you mean, "accident"?'

'Yes, both Zain and his elder brother, Khalid, were involved in a crash in... I believe they call it a *super car*.'

The buzz in Abby's head had got louder as the blood drained from her face...not just her face—even her oxygen-deprived fingertips tingled.

'I do not know the extent of the younger Prince's injuries but sadly his brother died, which means that the man you…*married*,' he gave a light laugh, 'is now the heir.'

'So how is…?' she'd paused, unable to reconcile the idea that her rescuer was also a royal prince, let alone put a name to the man who for so long had been anonymous '…he?' she'd finished weakly.

'The hospital is unwilling to reveal details to anyone but relatives.'

'Miss Foster?'

Abby started, her skittering glance moving from the Englishman to the two daunting figures in flowing Arab dress pretty much identical to those worn by the four who had shadowed her ever since she'd left her London apartment yesterday.

'I just want to confirm…you told no one, no one at all, about the…marriage document?'

'No one.' There had obviously been a lot of interest when she had had to recount the story but she'd played the kidnap down, preferring to turn the incident into a joke gone wrong rather than admit to the visceral, gut-churning nightmare it had been.

Her lashes flickered downwards as she ran her tongue across her lips to moisten them. She purposely kept her expression impassive even though inside her heart was thudding, the memory of visceral fear metallic on her tongue.

She pushed hard at the memory as she exerted control just as she'd practised. The memory belonged in another world a million miles from her own, where a disaster was a facial blemish—imagined or otherwise—that would spoil a fashion shoot.

'Excellent.' He turned his head as another robed figure approached. 'Will you excuse me?'

Abby watched as the men spoke for a few moments before Mr Jones returned. She had the immediate sense that under the emollient smile he was not happy.

'It seems that you may go in.' He gestured to the new arrival, who tipped his head in Abby's direction. 'Abdul will show you the way.'

'Aren't you coming in with me?' Abby asked, struggling to conceal her panic at the prospect of facing her 'husband' alone.

Beneath the little moustache the man affected, his lips thinned. 'It seems not.'

CHAPTER SIX

ABBY TOOK A deep breath, lifted her chin and walked through the door held by someone who looked more Security than medical, and who bowed low as she passed.

The soft, respectful murmur as she walked down the hallway seemed to be addressed to her. It would have been disconcerting had she had any thoughts to spare for anything but the question of what waited for her inside the room she was about to enter.

She slipped inside and as she closed the door behind her she hitched in a deep breath, straightened her shoulders and turned, wishing in that moment that she had asked more about Zain's condition. She had no idea what she was about to be confronted with—tubes, machines...was he even conscious?

Her sense of disorientation deepened as she found herself looking at what appeared to be an office, an office where a meeting seemed to be in progress at a long, rectangular table between several men wearing traditional Arab dress, and several more wearing business suits.

One of the men stood in front of what appeared to be a PowerPoint presentation, but moved towards Abby, who was already backing away mumbling apologies when he noticed her.

'Sorry. I think must be in the wrong...'

The man bowed and, after a momentary pause, the other men seated around the table got to their feet and followed his example.

This situation was just getting weirder, she thought, fighting the urge to curtsey or something.

'Not at all. This way, Amira...please...' His attitude deferential, he gestured for her to precede him towards a half-open door.

After a pause, she responded to the softly spoken invitation, even though as she approached the door the conviction that this was a case of mistaken identity grew stronger.

Then say something, idiot!

She half turned, ready to explain that this was a mistake, but her guide was backing out of the room with his head bent in a bow and it was hard to explain anything to someone you couldn't make eye contact with.

Her nerves were so stretched by this point that the soft sound of the door closing with a definitive click was enough to make her jump. Ignoring the chill of trepidation skittering down her spine, she turned.

This second room was not as large as the one she had entered, but still, was not small. It had the look of an upmarket hotel bedroom complete with a TV covering half of one wall and leather sofas around a glass coffee table covered with artistically stacked books.

The only thing that suggested she should not ring for Room Service was the hospital bed. It was empty, though the rumpled condition of the sheets and the drops of blood standing out against the white linen suggested it had been recently occupied by someone who had been attached to the bag of fluid that hung empty on a stand beside it.

She released a sigh, tried not to look at the blood and walked warily across the room towards the bed. Without thinking she put her hand on the sheets…they still retained the body heat of their recent occupant.

Abby clutched her head—all she wanted to do was get this over with and go home and she couldn't even find the man! 'Where the hell is he?' she murmured to herself.

'Behind you.'

At the sound of the soft, deep voice Abby jumped a foot off the floor as if a starting pistol had been unexpectedly fired in the room. She spun around, the action causing the silk veil on her head to slide off the slippery satin of her fiery curls.

She blinked and fought against the urge to retreat as the owner of the voice took a single step through a doorway that was half-concealed behind a screen and, without taking his eyes from her face, casually captured the fluttering fabric in his hand.

While his reflexes were clearly in excellent shape, Zain's bruised and battered body was not. Though he clenched his teeth against the pain zigzagging through his body as he straightened up, a muffled groan escaped his compressed lips.

The shock that had frozen her to the spot disappeared and was instantly replaced by concern. Abby laid a hand on his arm, her eyes widening as she registered the tense, rock-hard muscle through the fine fabric of his white shirt—more blood was spattered down one arm. Her stomach tightened before she looked away.

'Are you all right?'

Ah, well, someone always had to ask the stupid question. Might as well be her.

One hand pressed to his ribs, Zain lifted his eyelids and produced a look that managed to be both ironic and lazy through eyes that were every bit as blue as she remembered. They were shaded by lashes which looked almost ridiculously long and dark against the pallor that had robbed his vibrant, toned skin of its usual golden colour.

The memory of the first time she'd seen him floated into her head and, for a moment, the antiseptic room vanished and Abby was back in the desert encampment, the scent of woodsmoke and sour sweat almost as strong as the metallic taste of fear in her mouth.

At first she hadn't understood why the raucous cries and yells had faded, but then she'd seen the magnificence of the figure who rode into their midst, entirely ignoring the hostile stares and rifles aimed at him.

'Do I *look* all right?'

He looked incredible!

In that first startled moment when she had turned all she'd got was a blurred impression of the man she remembered—perfect face, perfect body and an aura of high-voltage *maleness* that had delivered a gut-punch blow to her unprepared nervous system.

'Should you be—?'

Standing there looking gorgeous?

Rising above the unhelpful prompting of her subconscious, she took a breath and tried again, focusing on the fact that, though her first impression was correct—he *was* still off-the-scale gorgeous—he also looked as though sheer willpower was the only thing keeping him on his feet.

'I decided that it might be hard to garner respect when any false move is likely to reveal my rear; however, getting dressed was not quite as simple as I thought.'

It was not his growled admission that brought a rush of colour to her cheeks but the mental image that flashed into her head. She was not in the habit of imagining men's bottoms…

'You could have asked someone for help…' Abby imagined that his position of power would make it likely that the staff would knock the door down to offer him assistance. 'Shall I…?' She paused and felt a flush bloom on her cheeks as she struggled to banish the half-formed image in her head of herself performing the required assistance…only in her mind she was taking the clothes off rather than helping him put them on.

'Shall I get someone to help you?'

'Someone who is not you?'

Her alarmed eyes flew to his face… *Relax, Abby; he can't read your mind.* 'One of those men in the—'

'No!' He barked out the injunction and then paused and took a deep, obviously painful breath before continuing in a more moderate tone. 'They are not nurses.'

'Who are they…? Sorry, I didn't mean to be nosy—'

'They are the men who run Aarifa.'

The comment shocked her into an uncensored response. 'Isn't that your father?'

'My father lost interest in the job a long time ago.'

Her curiosity was interlaced with empathy as an image of a frail and elderly ruler flashed into her head. 'So he relied heavily on your brother.'

The suggestion drew an odd laugh that terminated in another wince.

'I think I should call a nurse or—' Her concern morphed into something far less elevated when he lifted a hand, causing his unbuttoned shirt to gape open a few extra inches, revealing a hard, taut, muscle-ridged torso. The tendrils of shameful heat unfurling in the pit of her belly cooled into empathy as he winced and she realised his injuries were not restricted to his face.

Abby dragged her eyes upwards towards his face. Under the long-sleeved ankle-length silk dress she wore her heart continued to thud hard as she tilted her head back to meet his heavily lidded eyes. That in itself was a novelty—her own height meant it was rare that she ever had to look up at anyone.

'I think this is a mistake…' She stopped and shook her head. 'No, it *is* a mistake; I really don't know why I'm here…we could do this by email when you're feeling better, or…'

He placed a hand on the side of her cheek. The touch of his long fingers was light but the electrical tingle it sent through her nervous system was anything but.

'I prefer the personal touch.'

Abby fought the hypnotic tug of his electric-blue eyes and focused on the damage to his face, the bruising along the crest of one razor-sharp cheekbone that extended over the chiselled planes of his dramatically handsome face. Bruising that the dark shadow of stubble dusting his lean cheeks and angular jaw could not disguise.

'I don't.' She got nowhere near the level of cool she was aiming for but to her relief his hand fell away, though that may have been simply because he looked as though he needed all of his control just to stay standing up.

'Even if you manage to get dressed, you'll probably pass out...is that really worth it?'

An expression of hauteur spread across his lean features as he responded with chilly dismissal. 'I'm fine.'

'Well, you can be snooty if you like but I was only trying to help.'

The hauteur faded from his face, to be replaced by a smile that she found much more disturbing. 'As forthright as ever... I had forgotten.' His eyes slid from her face down her body, his gaze possessing a caressing quality that made her stomach muscles quiver. 'You scrub up rather well...'

She looked quickly away from the heat in his eyes, but not soon enough to stop the lick of flame that slid through her body.

'And it is very hard to tell that your feet are mismatched.'

Her wide eyes flew back to his face. 'You remember that?'

Something moved at the backs of his eyes. 'I remember everything.'

'You have a photographic memory?' she said, searching her own memory for any incriminating things she might have said.

He gave a low chuckle then stopped, lifting a supportive hand to his ribs. 'You take things very literally. I just meant that you are memorable.'

She lifted her chin. 'I'm assuming that's not a compliment.'

'It is a statement of fact. For a beautiful woman,' he observed, 'you seem to find taking a compliment graciously a struggle.'

The heat in his eyes was hard to escape, but then escaping when you didn't really want to was never going to be simple. It took her to the count of ten to regain control of her chaotic, jagged respirations. This was far too close and personal for her taste…injured or not, this man had a raw sexual aura that she found massively disturbing, but she had fought the hypnotic tug of his eyes before so she knew it was achievable if she tried.

Her confidence wilted when she lifted her eyes and found his gaze now trained on her mouth. While the heat low down continued to unfurl its very disturbing tendrils she fought to maintain a passive expression…or, at least, a *relatively* passive expression.

Zain quite literally couldn't stop staring at her mouth. He put down his lack of self-control to his weakened condition but in his head he saw that lush pinkness parting under the pressure he applied before he sank into…

The sabre-sharp stab of pain helped him distance himself from the sexual fantasies swirling in his head. Having her here was not about indulging his fantasies—it was far more prosaic.

His views on marriage had not changed but his position had. He was no longer the spare, he was the heir, and the forced desert marriage to this enticing redhead was all that stood between him and Kayla, who was waiting in the wings like a praying mantis in Prada.

He understood that continuity and the smooth transition of power was important, and he was fully prepared to accept the burden of duty that came with the role that he had been thrust into, a position the several people who he had awoken from the crash to find standing around his hospital bed had been eager to inform him of.

But, they added when several of the machines he was attached to had begun to beep loudly, he was not to concern himself with securing a bride. A wedding to his late brother's widow, a union that would ensure stability and the line of succession, could be performed as soon as he could leave his hospital bed.

He had felt the darkness coming to claim him and there had been no time for subtlety as he'd croaked out, 'I'm already married, Jones at the British Embassy will confirm.'

He had slept through the subsequent diplomatic storm his revelation had created, and by the time he'd been conscious again the marriage had been confirmed as genuine.

Abby had adopted a businesslike expression, though it was clear maintaining it was becoming difficult. 'So, is there something you want me to sign?'

'You're in a hurry.'

'The thing is, I think I'd prefer to get out of here before you kill yourself with all this unnecessary effort,' she husked out as her glance moved from his bloodstained shirt sleeve to the beads of moisture he could feel along his upper lip…and the deep lines of strain he knew were bracketing his mouth.

Her concern spilled over into exasperation. 'For heaven's sake, I know you're big and tough, but you're in pain. It doesn't make you a lesser man to admit it!' She rolled her eyes.

Her outburst startled him into silence but that quickly gave way to a low, throaty laugh. 'Fine, I'm not too proud to ask for help.' He nodded towards the bed. 'Will you lend me a shoulder?'

Abby's eyes were wide as she moved seamlessly from lofty female superiority to something approaching panic.

He lifted an arm. 'I'm swallowing my pride, and asking for your help.'

CHAPTER SEVEN

ABBY FOUND HERSELF staring at his abs, the muscles perfect enough to make her stomach flutter helplessly in reaction. She caught her lower lip between her teeth, disturbed more than slightly by her body's helpless reaction to his physicality.

It was mystifying and definitely bad timing! Lord, what was it about this man that made him the one member of the opposite sex capable of awakening her dormant sex drive? Recognising this was a question for later when she was safely back home and far away from temptation, so she huffed out a resigned but determined sigh and lifted her chin, responding to the internal challenge of not acting like a sex addict with as much dignity as she could manage.

'Fine. So what do you want me to do?'

He *almost* looked as if he was going to tell

her something very different, but at the last second he seemed to regain some control and dragged his eyes off her mouth. 'I just need to sit down for a minute.'

'All right, lean on me,' she said, trying to sound brisk and not breathless at the thought of contact with his hard, lean maleness.

'No, it's fine.'

She shot him a glance from under the sweep of her thick, straight lashes, discovering as she did that he was looking tense. 'You really don't have the hang of this accepting help thing, do you?' she sighed out. 'It was *your* idea,' she reminded him. 'And don't worry, I'm stronger than I look.'

An image of her landing a right hook on her captor's jaw flashed into her mind.

'I remember, *cara*,' he said, the look he gave her hinting that he was seeing the same replay in his own head.

The unexpected approving warmth in his voice brought a flush to her cheeks. 'I don't normally need rescuing,' she husked out, not sure why it felt important to establish this upfront, but it did.

The tentative half-smile that had begun to twitch the corners of her mouth upwards wilted then vanished completely as their glances connected. Abby had the weirdest sensation of time slowing as the air seemed to buzz with an invisible static. She had no idea how long the moment lasted, but when she did manage to wrench free she took refuge in resentment.

'Why didn't you tell me who you were?' Had it been some sort of joke to him? she wondered, remembering their smooth negotiation of the security checkpoints, which of course made perfect sense now.

'I was trying hard to forget myself.'

Abby had not begun to decipher this cryptic response when he moved in closer and laid a hand across her shoulders. She fought against the impulse to tense, the effort making her body quiver as she struggled to focus on the mundane, the ordinary, the smell of antiseptic to distract herself from the massive hormone rush that sent wave after wave of heat through her body.

Whether he was injured or not, the animal magnetism that poured off him had a mind-blanking force.

Get a grip, Abby told herself sternly as she followed her own advice, literally, and slid her arm very carefully around his narrow waist, feeling ludicrously self-conscious.

'Is that ok?' she asked, tilting her chin up to

look into his face. The veil of his lashes lifted and she was instantly skewered once more by the mesmeric tug of his electric-blue stare. When she managed, after a short delay, to react to his head jerk of acknowledgement, she was too flustered to notice that he looked as disconcerted as she felt.

She cleared her throat. 'Good, then lean on me and take your time…say when you need to stop.'

She hadn't wanted him to stop...

The memory surfaced and she felt a stab of shame. Oh, hell, now was *not* the time to relive a moment that was indelibly printed onto her mind for all the wrong reasons!

Her jaw quivered and her teeth clenched as she closed the door on the memory of the mortifying moment when she had come on to him with all the subtlety of a sledgehammer and then—as if that wasn't enough to make her cringe—been firmly rebuffed.

It was an embarrassing memory but that, she reminded herself, was all it was. It wasn't exactly rocket science—she'd been vulnerable and he hadn't taken advantage…humiliating at the time and, yes, she had hated him for it then, but now she was glad he'd been a gentleman.

Common sense told Abby that it had been

the circumstances as much as the man that had fanned into life instincts she didn't even know she possessed. Chances were she might never experience a moment like that again. She didn't know whether to be relieved or depressed by the thought.

At several points during the transfer his breathing sounded laboured but they didn't stop, their progress slow but steady.

'Thanks. I'll be fine now.' Zain straightened up and took the last steps under his own steam, then lowering himself down onto the edge of the bed. 'It's easing.'

She tossed him a sceptical look but shrugged; clearly, showing weakness was not his thing, another reason on the list she'd compiled that he really wasn't her type. The macho stuff really tried her patience; she liked men who didn't mind showing their vulnerable side. There was just one vital ingredient missing, however. The thought of kissing them, let alone anything more intimate, left her feeling…well, nothing really.

The silence stretched until Abby decided that getting straight to the point was probably the best policy—she knew what she wanted to say, as she'd been rehearsing it on the journey here, not sure when she'd have the opportunity to deliver her speech and wanting to be ready when it came.

'I wasn't sure if you'd be well enough for me to—'

He spread his hands in a mock-submissive gesture. 'I'm weak but willing.'

She cursed the flush that she felt run up under her skin but tried not to react to it. Being flippant was probably his way of coping; the man had almost lost his life and had seen his brother die, so having a fake wife revealed was the least of his problems but one she had no doubt he could do without.

She took a deep breath and decided that even though he was injured there was no point skirting delicately around the elephant in the room, and she could at least reassure him on some points. 'I just want you to know that I've no intention of…there is *no* question of me making any claims, if we really *are* married.' She paused, shaking her head slowly in an attitude of disbelief—she still couldn't quite believe they actually were. 'I'm assuming that under the circumstances an annulment will be straightforward. I can see what you're thinking.'

Well, that, Zain thought, made one of them!

'But you don't need to worry, I'll fully cooperate. I'll sign whatever you need me to sign,' she added earnestly. 'Including a confidentiality clause.' She pressed a finger to the small furrow between her brows as if mentally ticking things off a list. 'I don't think I've missed anything out.'

'Is your lawyer here with you?' Her expression was confirmation that she wasn't here to negotiate. She didn't, incredibly, seem to be aware that she had the advantage; she wasn't thinking about what she could get...she just wanted out.

'Do I *need* a lawyer?'

Everyone has an angle.

Zain had probably learnt this fact of life before he had had the ability to communicate it and now he had met someone who, it seemed, hadn't.

'And what sort of settlement did you have in mind for delivering these guarantees?' As he appealed to her avarice part of him *wanted* to see her fail the test, and silence the soft whisper of his freshly awoken optimism, but to his frustration Abigail Foster didn't even seem to recognise his gentle prompt; instead she reacted as though he'd just offered her an insult.

'Settlement...?' Her puzzled frown faded

as the angry heat climbed into her cheeks. '*Money*, you mean? I don't want anything from you!'

'Because such things are above you? You expect me to believe money means nothing to you?' he cut back. Nobody was that wholesome and sweet.

Her chin lifted but she didn't react to his challenge.

'I admire your principles' he said, a scornful curl turning his smile mocking. 'But are you really in the enviable position to refuse money?'

'You make it sound as though everything… everyone…is a commodity or has a price.'

'Oh, in my experience they do, *cara*, they do.'

'Then I pity you. I never want to be that cynical.'

'Don't get me wrong, I'm impressed, especially when you consider that you are supporting your grandparents.'

She went rigid, her delicate jaw quivering as her suspicious gaze narrowed on his face. 'Who told you that? What do you know about my grandparents?'

He produced an enigmatic smile that he saw made her teeth clench and intensified the uneasy look on her face.

'There should be no secrets between husband and wife.'

'I don't have any secrets.'

'True,' he drawled. 'The stories of your love life are pretty well-documented. And I'm assuming there has to be a built-in life expectancy to your kind of work.'

She'd gone on the huffy offensive to the suggestion she deserved to profit from the situation but the idea of losing her looks drew a laugh from her.

And he thought he knew women! This one seemed determined to challenge all his preconceptions.

'Before everything goes south, you mean,' she said cheerfully. 'Oh, I don't intend to stay in the job long enough for that to happen, just long enough to...' She broke off, giving a self-conscious shrug as her eyes slid from his. 'It's not my life's dream, I sort of fell into modelling. I was spotted at a shopping mall. I actually thought it was a set-up when the photographer approached me. I looked around for hidden cameras and told him the name on the card he gave me meant nothing to me.'

'I would have thought it was an obvious avenue for someone with your looks,' Zain observed, expelling a frustrated hiss from between clenched teeth as he gave up trying to fasten the button on his shirt. Apparently it took losing your healthy body to make a man appreciate having everything work. At least his debilitation was temporary, he thought, sending up a silent prayer of thanks for that.

'You mean the height,' she held a hand flat on top of her head, 'and *the* face?' She gave a gurgle of laughter.

The attractive sound brought his attention zeroing in on that face, and this time he felt not only his libido stir, which it had done the moment he laid eyes on the supple curves of her luscious body, but also his curiosity. He was forced to accept the seemingly impossible— that there was nothing feigned about her lack of vanity and yet she worked in an industry where looks were everything.

His eyes drifted down the long lines of her superb body. 'You don't seem to take your looks very seriously.'

'If I'd taken my looks seriously I'd be...' She paused and brought her lashes down in a protective sweep before adding lightly, 'I was five-ten at twelve years old. My nickname was freak or giraffe. As for my face,' her fingers moved lightly across the delicately angled features, 'someone said I looked like their cat and it kind of followed me, not that I expect you to understand,' she said without heat—people couldn't help the way they looked, and he probably didn't even realise that he made other men feel insecure, especially other men with wives, she mused, not struggling at all to imagine the effect he had on her own sex.

She was just grateful that she possessed the ability to consider her own reaction to his sexual aura with objectivity... *Yeah, you carry on telling yourself that, Abby.*

'Why wouldn't I understand?'

She resisted the temptation to dodge the question while she endured the heat as a flush travelled up her neck, but delivered her reply with as much composure as she could manage.

'Because I'm doubting you were ever an ugly duckling, Prince...is that what I call you...?'

'You call me Zain.'

Abby suppressed the childish impulse to tell him she didn't want to call him anything, she wanted to go back home.

'You think of yourself that way? As an ugly duckling?'

Abby was thrown enough by the question to miss a beat. Yes, she supposed deep down,

no matter how other people saw her, she was
still the ugly duckling. It was ironic really
that what had set her apart at school had been
the reason for her success. The length of her
neck or her legs was no longer mocked but
admired… 'Have I wandered into a therapy
session?' How, she wondered, had this conversation got so personal so quickly?

'Aha!' He pounced on her response. 'It's
classic avoidance technique, answering a question with a question.'

A much better technique in her experience
was to pretend she didn't understand the joke,
especially when *she* was the joke. It was the
only way to prevent the outside world realising
they were getting to her…to that end she'd cul-
tivated a mask, the same mask that was much
in demand at photo shoots, only now they
called it enigmatic.

And Zain's reference to her love life being
well-documented… She had her agent to thank
for that, leaking stories about her 'romances'
on social media, because, as she put it, *'Abby,
darling. you're as dull as ditchwater, and beg-
gars can't be choosers. You're not one of the
elite… Relax. It's win-win and you'll get the
odd free dinner out of it.'*

The romances were usually with male celebrities who needed the publicity because their career had dipped or younger, media-hungry newbies out to make their mark. It was all part of her image.

'Sorry to disappoint you but I'm not a needy basket case. I always had a warm home to go back to at the end of a bad day.'

'So what did your parents think of your career move?'

'My grandparents,' she corrected, her brow pleating as she recalled his earlier comment. 'My parents died when I was very young and Nana and Pops supported my decision because they understood that I didn't want to leave uni with a massive debt. I wanted to be financially independent.' And after Gregory's betrayal her modelling career had been the lifeline that had helped keep her virtually penniless grandparents afloat.

'It was a hard time for them, though, when I first started out. They were swindled out of their life savings and pensions.' She swallowed as she felt her throat thicken with tears. 'An investment in a project,' she continued in a flat voice that she hoped revealed none of the devastation and frustration and guilt she still felt, 'that never existed and a financial advisor who vanished off the face of the earth.'

His expression was thoughtful as he listened to her. 'You're really very good, aren't you, at pretending it doesn't hurt?'

Her eyes fluttered wide in shock before she coaxed a laugh from her aching throat. 'Are you always this sure of your infallibility or is it the medication? Speaking of which…' Her concern became genuine as she scanned his face; the bruises seemed to have deepened in colour since she'd been in the room, which, now that she thought of it, had to have been a long time ago. 'I should be going…'

'Where?'

It was a good question.

'You missed out one thing in your story. It was your boyfriend who scammed them and stole their life savings.'

Her face flamed with shocked guilt before the colour fled, leaving her lily-pale. 'Have you got a file on me in a drawer somewhere?'

'In a safe.'

He said it so casually that her jaw dropped.

Zain took advantage of her dumbstruck silence. 'I have a proposition to put to you. How would you like to be in a position to buy back your grandparents' bungalow and restore their savings?'

He really did know everything! 'I fully intend to…' She shook her head. 'You have a *file* on me…?' Her eyes flashed with outrage.

He registered that outrage suited her but didn't allow his appreciation to divert him. 'I don't mean in a year or two years, I mean now, today.'

'Is that meant to be some sort of joke?' Expression stony, she pointed to her face. 'Not sure if you'd noticed, but I'm not laughing.'

'Eighteen months of your life.'

'Eighteen months doing what?' she tossed back.

'Being my wife.'

The moment of dumbstruck silence was followed by her shaky laughter as she said in a flat voice, 'I think you have a fever.'

'Not every woman in the world would consider being my wife such a horrifying prospect.'

'Can't imagine what the attraction is unless…oh, let me think…maybe the life of luxury, the private jet, the holidays…not that I'm judging.'

'Yes, I can tell.' He smiled as the sarcasm earned him another flash from her magnificent emerald eyes. 'Look, just hear me out, and then make an…objective decision based on the facts and not on your emotional reaction. As for marriage, we are both on the same page—I don't want to be married any more than you do.'

Her delicate brows arched. 'Not ever?'

As his eyes swivelled her way it was clear that she regretted having betrayed her curiosity.

'Not ever,' he said flatly. 'However, my situation requires that, as my father's heir, I am married. In this situation, custom would normally dictate that after my brother's death my bride would be his widow.'

It took her a few seconds to process this information. 'That's positively...' The idea of asking a grieving woman to be passed on like a worn-out pair of shoes evoked a response strong enough to lend a sheen of emotion to her eyes. 'Oh, my God...poor woman.'

'Exactly.'

'But you won't, will you...do that to her?'

'I will do everything within my power to prevent this from happening, but it's not just about me; the solution is in your hands.'

'Mine...?'

'Well, if I am already married, Kayla will escape this terrible fate.'

'That's not fair,' she protested at his not at all well-disguised display of moral blackmail.

'Life is not fair; however, I am offering a practical solution, not asking you to bear my children.'

She flushed and pushed away from him.

'I never thought you were,' she assured him with a disdain that didn't fully hide her embarrassment.

'You're not the first person to be taken in,' he began, responding to a need to offer her some comfort that was alien to his nature. 'You really shouldn't beat yourself up about what happened to your grandparents.'

She read the pity in his comment and reacted with anger. 'Like you'd know anything about it!'

'Fine, carry on berating yourself.' He gave an offhand shrug, unwilling to admit even to himself that the conflict shining in her beautiful eyes stirred something inside him. 'Or, alternatively, you could swallow your pride and accept this offer.' Zain watched as she stiffened and bit down on her full lower lip, her teeth digging into the soft, pink plumpness. Her lashes brushed her smooth cheek as she glanced down but he could see the resentment sparkling through the dark filigree.

* * *

'Offer or ultimatum?' she charged, thinking *temptation* might be a more accurate description.

'It benefits us both.'

'It would change my life.' It would also change her grandparents' lives—could she ever look at them knowing that she could have given them back the retirement they had planned and saved for and hadn't?

Could she look at herself?

He didn't bother denying her assertion. 'Yes, your life will change.'

Abby could feel her resistance fading but she clung on, not prepared to concede just yet. 'Isn't a scandal the thing you want to avoid?' If their desert marriage was revealed there was going to be one and she was going to be at the centre of it. Saying yes would mean saying goodbye to any semblance of a private life for the next year and a half...could she cope with that? 'Or are you suggesting people aren't going to notice my sudden appearance?'

His eyes moved from her vivid face to her auburn hair. 'These situations can be managed,' he assured her smoothly. 'There are people whose job it is to put a positive spin on anything.'

An image of her future life of endless ceremony and presence flashed before her eyes, and it was followed immediately by an equally vivid picture of her grandparents pottering around the garden of their bungalow with a front door that didn't have six bolts on it.

'I wish—' she began.

He cut across her, his tone sardonic. 'I'm sure that his wife wishes my brother were not dead.'

Abby felt a stab of guilty contrition—she'd been so self-absorbed that she hadn't even considered how he must be feeling—and her mouth twisted in a grimace of self-condemnation.

'I am truly sorry.' Belated but better than not at all, she gave her condolences, not that he seemed to recognise them as such.

'Sorry?' he echoed, his dark eyes drawn into an interrogative line above his nose.

'About your brother,' she explained awkwardly.

'Oh…' he grunted as he eased one long leg onto the bed and then the other, murmuring a soft word of thanks when she pushed a couple of pillows under his head, her tummy quivering in sympathy at the sight of the bruises on the golden expanse of his stomach.

His eyes were closed and for a moment she thought he'd fallen asleep, and she was thinking about creeping away when he opened them again; the electric-blue had a febrile quality.

'We weren't close,' he revealed.

'But he was your brother.' She'd always wanted a sibling and had envied the big, noisy family who lived next to her grandparents.

'Half-brother,' he corrected, closing his eyes again. 'So do we have a deal?'

She glanced up from her contemplation of her clenched fists. 'I need to think.'

'Fine.' He closed his eyes.

The tension had barely begun to leave her bunched shoulders when he spoke again.

'Let me know what you decide in two minutes.'

His eyes opened, the glazed glow in the blue depths doing nothing to ease her stress levels.

'I didn't come here to…to…stay married, I came here to disentangle our—'

'Past, present, future?'

'We don't have a *future*.' They both heard the questioning upward inflection in the last word.

'Eighteen months. That's all I ask.'

Abby, the conflict clearly written on her face, shook her head in a slow negative motion. 'No… I can't.' An image of her grandparents floated into her head with their brave smiles, noisy neighbours and no garden. Pops had so loved his garden.

Her shoulders dropped in defeat as she took the step that sent her over the cliff edge she had been balancing on.

'Yes, all right, I'll do it.' The moment she spoke she knew it was the right, the *only* response she could have given, but it didn't stop her feeling sick, literally.

Hand pressed to her mouth, she turned away, in her haste stumbling over the trailing wires that must at some point have been attached to Zain.

That was when the bells started ringing!

CHAPTER EIGHT

'Sorry… Sorry… How do I turn it off…?' Abby picked up the loops of wire she'd sent flying and looked at the space-age machine lit up by red flashing lights.

Before Zain could respond to her frantic question the first white-coated figure burst through the door, several more followed in quick succession and the sheer volume of people pushed a bewildered Abby against a wall, where she stood watching as Zain responded to the medical attention with increasing irritation.

He raised his voice to be heard above the din of the alarms and the medical babble. 'I'm not dead—the fact I'm breathing is the first clue. Will someone please turn that damned thing off?'

The sudden cessation of noise created a freeze-frame moment. Zain broke the silence to order the rapid departure of all the white coats and before she knew it Abby and Zain were alone once again.

'Sorry about that.' She lifted her chin in challenge. 'I'm very clumsy.' Surely he could see now that she was not princess material.

'I noticed. Do you fall off the catwalk often?'

'I'm a professional.'

'Then direct the same professionalism to our contract and there will be no problem.' He gestured towards the chair she had just vacated.

She didn't accept the invitation but stood there, her hands clasped across her stomach and her brow pleated with a furrow of consternation. 'You know this is crazy—people are never going to believe...' Her hand moved in a descriptive arc from him to herself. 'Nobody will believe that *we* are married.'

'Why not? It's true.'

A tiny flicker of a smile moved shadow-like across her face. 'There were times when I convinced myself I dreamt it.' Her chest lifted in a tiny little sigh of resignation. 'So how would it work? What are you going to tell people?'

'How *will* it work?' he emphasised, before adding with some of the hauteur she remembered from their previous encounter, 'My father is the only person I am required to *explain* myself to, and I will explain to him that you are my soulmate.' His expressive lips curved into a cynical half-smile that left his eyes cold as he continued to reveal their fictional back story. 'We fell in love, and there was a falling-out; I shall be vague on this but we are both, you see, passionate people and so these things happen…then the news of my accident had you rushing to my side because you realised that your life was nothing without me.'

'You should write fiction…or fairy stories,' she husked back.

'Any good writer knows you target your story to your audience.' His voice carried no discernible inflection but the cynicism in his azure stare was painfully pronounced as he explained, 'My father is a firm believer in fairy tales. Are you?'

Unprepared for the abrupt and vaguely accusing addition, she looked confused. 'Am I what?'

'A believer in fairy tales, *cara*?' he drawled.

She clenched her teeth. 'What if I am? It's not a crime,' she shot back. 'And will you stop calling me that—has someone told you Italian makes you sound sexy or something? For the record, it doesn't!' she lied.

After a startled silence his low, husky laughter rang out. 'I wasn't aware I was using it; I've recently spent some time with my mother…the language kind of rubs off.' The long weekend in Venice had turned into a fortnight when the diva had been forced to cancel a booking at the Met due to a throat infection which she had been convinced was about to end her career. Her harassed, much younger live-in lover had been unable to cope with the dramatic declarations that her career was over and so had begged Zain to extend his stay.

Zain had taken pity on the guy because he'd lasted longer than most, and his mother was nobody's idea of low-maintenance.

'Your mother is Italian?' Her brow speared into a speculative furrow. 'Spend some time…?' Her eyes flickered wide. 'Does that mean—?'

'She left when I was eight.'

'She left you?' Abby struggled not to sound shocked at the idea.

'She considered it the unselfish thing to do.' There was no inflection in his voice but the twist of his lips was ironic as he explained his parent's motivation. 'She could no longer deprive the operatic world and her public of her talent.'

Had she *really* said that to a little boy…? Abby couldn't bring herself to ask…she wasn't sure what shocked her most about the story—the seeming total lack of maternal feeling or the impression of total self-absorption.

'So, you see, Italian is quite literally my mother tongue. Most people here in Aarifa speak French and Arabic and a good percentage speak English as well these days, though there are some schools that are giving Mandarin preference. So, to business. If you give Hakim the details of your grandparents' account I will have the funds deposited by the end of the day.'

'From a hospital bed?'

'It is called delegation…*cara*.'

The addition was deliberate but her stomach gave a little kick anyway. 'You've got this planned but aren't you missing the details? You haven't asked how much my grandparents need.'

'Then tell me.'

She took a breath and said the sum she was short of for the house purchase and her grandparents' pension pot very quickly, but it still sounded an awful lot. She looked at him warily through her lashes.

'Per week, it sounds reasonable.'

She looked him as though he were mad. 'Week!' she yelped. 'Are you insane?'

He shook his head. 'I really hope you have an agent for your modelling work, otherwise you'd be paying them.'

Abby watched as he reached for the phone that lay on the locker beside the bed and punched in a number while she stood there wondering what the hell she had signed herself up for as he spoke quickly to someone at the other end.

'Well, that is organised,' he said, sliding seamlessly into English as he finished the call. 'Hakim has just arrived at the hospital. He was bringing me some personal items,' he added by way of explanation. 'He will escort you back, and have Layla, my housekeeper, settle you in.'

'Take me back where?'

He looked surprised by the question. 'To the palace.'

'Right now…?' Panic gave her question a shrill edge.

'What if I see someone, what do I say, and Mr Jones is waiting…he…?'

'I will attend to Mr Jones, and I imagine you will see several people. None of them will ask you any difficult questions; they are there to make you comfortable. If you need anything just ask Hakim.'

'You're not giving me time to think,' she protested weakly. 'And who is Hakim?'

As if on cue there was a knock on the door before it opened to reveal a man who was so broad you didn't immediately notice he was not above average height.

'This is Hakim, my right hand.'

Excluded as Zain slid into what appeared to be a mixture of Arabic and French—presumably he was issuing instructions because the other man nodded several times—it wasn't until after Zain had finished speaking that Hakim turned and bowed his head once again, this time to her.

'I hope you will enjoy your stay with us, Your Royal Highness.'

'Thank you...' Her glance skittered towards Zain lying in the bed— his position did not stop him manipulating everyone like some sort of chess master but her little blip of resentment faded as she saw the lines of fatigue around his eyes.

'You should get some sleep,' she scolded, missing the thick-set man's startled expression when she added sternly, 'And don't do anything really stupid like getting out of bed!'

Zain did close his eyes after the door closed... and lay there wondering if he'd done something very stupid. Did she have the faintest clue of what she had agreed to?

Though present, the doubts tinged with guilt flickering through his head did not last. Doubts were a luxury, a weakness he could not afford. Opposing a forced marriage to Kayla and making enemies along the way would expend time and energy he also could not afford. His father may have lost sight of the fact that in their position of privilege a personal life must always be secondary to duty, but Zain had not.

He knew it was essential that, as heir apparent, he must establish his authority without delay if he was to stand any chance of bringing about the reform the country needed.

And it did need it.

Always held up as a shining example of liberal thinking and progress over the past few years, Aarifa, without a strong figurehead, was increasingly becoming a country run on a system of patronage and tribal alliances between the ruling families. Corruption was already rampant and worst of all it was becoming an accepted business practice. Zain had watched from the sidelines, painfully aware of the decline but impotent as the younger son to do anything to prevent what was happening. He had watched while the country's oil wealth was siphoned off into tax-haven accounts, while the growing inequality caused discontent and unrest.

For those who would resist his reforms Zain knew the scandal of his mother would resurface and they would try to smear him by association. There was nothing he could do about that but he could stop them weaponising his single state. A temporary marriage of convenience was the obvious solution even if that did mean throwing Abby Foster into the palace life of intrigue and deception...how would she cope?

He ground his teeth as he brushed away the question but not before his thoughts had been infiltrated by guilt once more. She would not lose out by this situation, he reminded himself, and in eighteen months when he had established his authority she would be free to take up her life once more without the burden of debt hanging over her head. She would have the freedom to choose, something that Zain knew he had lost in the moment of his brother's death.

He dug his head a little deeper into the pillow and reached behind his head with a grunt of effort to switch off the oxygen and the irritating hiss. Settling back, he closed his eyes.

Behind his flickering eyelids his thoughts continued to swirl until he closed them down, refusing to allow emotions to rule his actions the way his father always had. He fell asleep not thinking of reform but of a woman with green eyes smiling at him while she wrapped her fiery hair and her slim arms around his body.

CHAPTER NINE

YOU THOUGHT THIS was a good idea why, *exactly?* Abby asked herself as the door finally closed behind Layla. She resisted the temptation to open it to see if the two large men were still stationed there… Were they to keep people out or to keep her in…?

It didn't really matter though; the idea of anyone making it this far into a building that had a dizzying number of corridors and discreet but visible security was laughable. Though really, even if intruders got in they would never find their way out…there were probably skeletons of would-be thieves and assassins gathering dust in unknown marble-floored corners of the building even now.

She was too tired to smile at the fantasy image as the weariness, both mental and physical, went cell-deep. Even a cursory view of one of the bathrooms—the suite had two—did not tempt her to do more than brush her teeth and splash water on her face.

She stepped out of her borrowed dress, leaving it where it dropped. She could imagine her grandmother's horror at such slovenly behaviour but was too tired to do anything more than pull her nightshirt over her head before flinging herself face down on the bed where someone had conveniently pulled back the silk sheets.

She had never seen a bed this big, let alone slept in one. Despite its size it actually looked small in her vast room, which was part of a suite of similarly palatial rooms, but then it was a *palace*.

Perhaps she could ask to be moved to something a little cosier tomorrow, if this place even did cosy…? She was still debating the question when sleep claimed her. She dreamt of the enormous bed she lay in but in her dreams she wasn't alone…

As she emerged from a deep sleep the next morning the dreams that had dominated her night slipped away, leaving just an impression, an odd ache deep inside her and a tight feeling in her chest. As these too slipped away she experienced a moment's total disorientation that tipped over into panic as she stared at the in-

tricately coloured antique-glass panels in the
delicately wrought brass chandelier that hung
over the bed.

'Where am…?'

Then she remembered, the previous day's
events trickling through her head like an old-
fashioned slide show. With a groan she sat bolt
upright, giving a startled gasp when she saw
the young woman standing a few feet away
holding a tray.

The girl's smile slipped a little, but who
could blame her being scared, Abby reflected,
as her morning look tended towards super-
scary even on good days? It didn't matter how
successfully she tamed her hair during the day,
at night it went its own wild way, and, as she
had no memory of removing any make-up last
night, she probably had panda-eyes as well.

'Good morning…you startled me.' Just as
well her tenure in the palace was temporary
because she wouldn't like to think of this as
part of her morning routine…of course, Zain's
real wife might enjoy a very different sort
of morning routine. She might wake beside,
maybe even entangled with… Abby's eyes half
closed and her head extended to one side as
she imagined lips moving up the curve of her
neck, tracing a sensual path to her mouth. The

kiss would be deep and slow, hungry… Her eyes shot open as she sucked in a guilty gasp through flared nostrils.

What are you doing, Abby?

A burn of shame joined the other burn already lit low in her belly and she responded to the young woman's question of, 'Coffee?'

'Lovely, thank you.'

The girl sketched a little curtsey, put the tray on a table a few feet away and turned back.

'The curtains…?' she asked, nodding to the row of four floor-length windows along the opposite wall, all covered by heavily embroidered curtains.

Abby nodded and lifted a self-conscious hand to her hair as she pulled back the sheet and swung her legs over the edge of the bed. The cartoon cat grinning on her chest tugged her lips into a twisted smile—her nightwear looked almost as incongruous in these surroundings as she felt!

That feeling didn't diminish when the young woman approached with a floor-length dressing gown in oyster silk. They probably stocked such luxury items in a selection of sizes on the off-chance that an overnight guest might need one.

Or maybe one of Zain's *personal* overnight

guests had left it behind? The fabric might have been impregnated with this faceless woman's perfume... The idea took hold and seemed so strong that Abby found herself taking a step backwards, the young attendant's face making her realise that her own expression must be reflective of the deep repugnance she was experiencing.

She dug deep and forced a smile, standing still as the younger woman slid the gown over her arms. Thankfully it smelt of nothing but *newness*. Frowning faintly, Abby stepped away, fastening the belt around her slim waist and wondering why she had overreacted so much to the hardly surprising idea that Zain slept with women; it would have been naive... actually insane to assume he didn't have an active sex life.

What would have been surprising would be the discovery that he lived the life of a monk. She smiled at the thought, ignoring the inexplicable nauseous knot that still lingered in her belly.

His sex life was not of any interest to her, she told herself, but what *was* of interest to her was the question of whether he intended to continue enjoying his bachelor lifestyle for the next eighteen months...yes, her interest in that was totally legitimate, she decided with some relief.

If she was expected to play her part this was exactly the sort of information she needed. If she was expected to look the other way and pretend she didn't know about his affairs it would be good to know ahead of time what the royal etiquette for that would be.

Oh, yeah, Abby, that should be a really good Q&A session. What would be a good opening line...? I'm not interested in who you sleep with, but...

She spared a moment of sympathy for his real wife when he took one, though she supposed there was any number of women in the world willing to make quite a lot of compromises to occupy the position she had temporarily found herself in.

The knowledge would have been easier to live with if she had been able to pretend that it was his position, his status and conspicuous wealth that attracted these faceless women who in her head were stepping over each other to offer themselves to him, but Abby knew that, even stripped of all the trappings of his position, Zain had more earthy sex appeal in his little finger than any man on the planet.

She sucked in a breath, dispelling the disturbing image forming in her head. 'Too much stripping, Abby.'

The expression of the petite woman who had been holding out the gown was wary as she shook her head to signal she didn't understand what Abby had said.

'Don't worry, I'm mad but not dangerous.'

The girl, continuing to look wary, held out a pair of slippers, delicate little velvet things embroidered with open toes and a tiny wedge heel.

Abby didn't realise her intention until the girl was about to drop down to her knees, and at this point she snatched the slippers and slid her feet into them herself. 'Perfect fit...' Abby arched a delicate brow of enquiry in the younger woman's direction.

'Mina,' the young woman supplied shyly as she dragged her curious gaze from Abby's flamed hair, which seemed to fascinate her.

'Thanks, Mina, but I can take it from here,' Abby said politely but firmly.

It took a few attempts but Abby finally managed to convey her message, namely that she didn't need help to dress, drink or anything else. It had taken five minutes and Abby was on her second cup of reviving strong coffee by the time she walked the younger woman to the door, where she received a startled look in response to her casual parting shot of *see you later.*

'Morning, guys!' she called to the men standing outside before ducking back in.

She leaned against the wall, thought *steep learning curve* and began to laugh…hysteria, she told herself as the tears ran down her cheeks. Ah, well, as her nan would have said, better to laugh than cry. She might have entered into a very dubious deal with a sinfully good-looking devil who, pointless to pretend otherwise, she was not immune to, but it was a means to an end and she'd make it clear when she saw him that she was probably going to mess up…royally! She dragged a hand though her tousled hair and wondered when she was likely to see him and what she was meant to do in the meantime.

Zain had seemed convinced that he'd be discharged from hospital today but that seemed unrealistic to Abby.

Floating in a bath into which she had tipped half a gallon of truly glorious-smelling oil from one of the crystal flagons on the marble-topped washstand, she began to feel slightly more relaxed.

She didn't manage to empty her mind but at least she had things more in perspective—

a few uncomfortable months of her life was a price worth paying to know that her grandparents would be able to live in comfort for the rest of theirs.

She had just emerged from the decadent sunken tub and was towelling herself dry when she heard the sound of voices. She took a deep breath, wrapped a towel turban-style around her hair and tightened the sash on the silk robe. Clearly she had not convinced the woman that she could cope alone.

She took a deep breath, realising she'd just have to be blunt. 'Thank you, Mina, but I'm—'

The level of calm she'd achieved in the bath went flying out of the window. Mina was there, along with two other women, one of whom was folding items of clothing that were definitely not Abby's into a tall chest of drawers, removing layers of tissue paper as she did so. The other was helping Mina fill a wardrobe with hanger-hung items which all had labels still attached.

This was all disturbing but it was a gnat bite to a mountain lion when compared with the disturbing presence of the man who was standing there supervising them!

CHAPTER TEN

SHOCK HELD HER immobile but was it shock that made her body hum or that made the silk suddenly feel heavy against her sensitised nerve-endings?

In no mood to think about alternative explanations to shock, she caught her lower lip between her teeth, lifted her chin and waited for him to acknowledge her presence, and in the seconds it took she made a comprehensive survey of his tall, dynamic figure, casual in beautifully cut dark trousers and a pale open-necked shirt that didn't make him any less of a dauntingly elegant figure or lessen the impact of his sheer male physicality.

There was nothing that even vaguely suggested his invalid status. The bruises she knew were on his body were concealed and with his left profile presented to her the damage to his face was hidden.

He turned his head then and Abby pulled in a tense breath as their eyes clashed electric-blue on emerald. After a moment that seemed to stretch on for ever he tipped his head in curt acknowledgement.

Breathing again, she watched as he turned back to the women, said something that had them dropping curtsies and murmuring a respectful chorus of *'Amir!'* before they hurried from the room, eyes down.

Zain waited until the door had closed and then he waited some more before he turned back; it took the extra moments to get his rampaging libido back under some sort of control. Being celibate for too long went some way to explaining the strength of his reaction...some, but not all.

It was crazy and he'd never known anything like it. It had been the slither of silk that had initially alerted him to her presence and sent the rush of aroused heat through his body, the rush becoming a flood when he'd turned and got his first look at her, sinuous curves swathed in silk that clung to her breasts and the long, lovely line of her shapely thighs. It was obvious she didn't have a stitch on underneath.

He lifted his gaze quickly, but not quickly enough to stop the painful pulse of heat from skewering him where he stood. She had the body of a goddess, athletic and toned.

The effort of dragging his eyes upwards caused the muscles along his jaw to quiver. He forced his hands to unclench; the sensation of not being in complete control of himself was a new one—one he didn't like. Thankfully he recognised it for what it was—simple sexual desire.

'Should you be out of hospital?' Abby sounded shrill.

'I have been given a clean bill of health.'

'Who did you bully and intimidate into signing that?' She couldn't resist the retort but as he held her gaze he sensed she immediately regretted it. A long, uncomfortable moment passed before he spoke.

'Is that some subtle allusion…are you trying to suggest that I *bullied* you, Abigail?'

'Nobody calls me Abigail.' She shook her head and sighed. 'All right, this is my decision. I've agreed to do this but—'

'Ah, the *but*…?'

'I don't think I can carry it off.'

'I don't see the problem.'

Her mouth twisted at his unsympathetic response. It was plain that she found it extremely frustrating that he didn't seem to take her concerns seriously.

'That is the problem—you don't. The girl earlier—she tried to put my *shoes* on!' Her voice rose to an incredulous quiver that made his lips twitch.

His glance dropped to her painted toes peeking out through the velvet before returning to her face. 'And that is a problem because?'

'See?' she said, lifting her hands in a point-proven gesture. 'Having people put your shoes on for you is normal for you; for me it's…well, ridiculous, and it makes me feel uncomfortable.'

'It is not compulsory; I have been known to tie my own shoelaces on occasion.'

'You're laughing at me!' she accused hotly.

He huffed out a grunt that could be construed as apology or maybe an admission. 'I appreciate this all might seem strange to you at first.'

'Big of you,' she said, refusing to be mollified.

'I have every confidence that you will fulfil your side of the deal, unless I read you wrong?'

He watched her eyes narrow at the suggestion she was not a woman of her word, and tough to boot, which was the response he had intended.

'I said I'd do this and I will.' The words carried more conviction with an image of her grandparents in her head. 'Obviously I will need to speak to my agent.' He wasn't going to be happy she had work commitments lined up. 'I don't know what I'm going to say to him.' Whatever she said it would be difficult to defend herself against his inevitable accusation of lack of professionalism.

'I'll sort it—give me the name.'

Her lips tightened. 'I don't want *you* to *sort* it.' She cinched the belt on her robe another defiant notch. 'Look, this,' her fluttering gesture took in their surroundings, 'isn't public so I don't have to pretend to be weak and ineffectual. I am more than capable of sorting my own affairs. Obviously in public I will do my best to act as though I think every word you utter is a pearl of wisdom, but in private—'

'In private,' he drawled, 'you will assert your independence just for the hell of it. Sounds like a fun eighteen months. For the record, I was simply trying to smooth things for you, not take over your life.'

'I think you've already done that, considering you *saved* my life,' she admitted. Abby caught her full lower lip between her teeth and pushed out a husky, 'I know… I know it's my choice and I will try not to keep hitting you on the head with it,' she promised. 'My grandparents taught me to take responsibility for my own actions…' Her face fell, a look of dismay widening her eyes. 'Oh, God, Nana and Pops!' How was she going to explain this to them?

'Whatever you want to tell your grandparents, I will go along with it.'

Taken aback by his concession and his quick reading of the situation, shee took a moment to respond. 'I don't know what I'm going to tell them…maybe I don't have to tell them yet— it's two weeks before they get back from their cruise. And delaying the inevitable seems very attractive just now.'

His brows hit his dark hairline, taking her glance with them, and her eyes stayed glued to the blond streak that he knew stood out against the glossy black.

He caught the direction of her stare and lifted a hand to his head. 'My mother come from Northern Italy. There are a lot of blondes there, though she is a redhead these days.' His brow furrowed. '*Cruise…?* I thought that your grandparents were strapped for cash?'

'They are but they won a competition in

a magazine that my nan didn't even remember entering…an all-expenses-paid trip in the Caribbean,' she said, looking anywhere but at him…the woodwork over the door was really quite marvellous.

'There was no competition, was there?'

She dragged her eyes away from the doorway. 'What makes you say that? Of course… oh, all right, then, there wasn't, but Pops got really ill starting last winter; he had bronchitis and it really wore him down, so the summer was a total washout.' She looked at him, her chin tilted to a defiant angle. 'Then I saw this cruise advertised—it was massively reduced, they were virtually giving it away to fill empty cabins, and I knew they wouldn't let me pay so I invented the competition,' she admitted, fixing him with a so-hang-me glare.

'So you *can* lie.' Very badly, as it happened. 'There's no need to look so guilty. It was a kind thing to do.'

Her dark eyelashes fluttered against her cheek as she experienced a glow of pleasure that was totally disproportionate to the unexpected praise.

'Have you eaten?'

She nodded and looked across to the table

where she'd sat earlier, but the dishes had already vanished, along with last night's fresh flowers, which had been replaced by an equally fabulous arrangement of beautiful blooms. The place seemed to be populated by an army of people whose job it was to wait on her hand and foot without her ever seeing them.

'Good, then get dressed and we can be off.'

She blinked and stood her ground even though having one layer of silk between her skin and his eyes made her feel quite ridiculously exposed, and clothes—a wool jumper or something equally covering—seemed a very good idea!

'Off where?'

'I thought I'd give you the guided tour.'

'That's really not necessary,' she said, wondering why he would offer to show her around himself when anyone else in his position would delegate.

He raised a brow and folded his long length into one of the easy chairs set beside the double French doors that opened out onto a balcony. 'What are you planning to do? Stay in here?'

'Why not? A family of six could live here comfortably and I could do with catching up on some reading.' She gave a sigh and added,

'Look, I think that, under the circumstances, it would be better that I keep a low profile.'

'That would defeat the object of this exercise.'

She pursed her lips and tilted her head to one side, angling a feathery brow. 'And that was again…?'

'Showing that the future ruler of Aarifa has a beautiful wife which makes him a strong and dependable pair of hands. The press office have issued a statement this morning.'

'Already!' She fought her way through the panic churning in her stomach. 'So what is expected of me—do I speak or just wear clothes and smile?' The latter ought to be fine…it was just about all she'd done with her life so far, she thought, stifling a slug of resentment. When he came to choose a bride for real, would he want a mannequin then too or a real woman?

'I think wearing clothes is a good idea,' he said with an amused, sensual grin. 'I hope there are some you care for in what I've ordered, but feel free to order anything else you need or want.'

'Where did they all come from?'

'I couldn't tell you exactly, I just gave your measurements to—'

'My measurements? How did you know my measurements?'

A slow smile split his lean face as his glance slid slowly over her slim, sinuous curves. 'I have a good eye for such things, *cara*.'

'And no doubt a lot of practice sizing up women,' she flung back, focusing on the annoyance of him making her blush, rather than the fire zigzagging along the nerve endings under the surface of her skin.

'Oh, and for the shoes I got two sizes of each to accommodate your feet.' He looked down at the items under discussion. 'Shall I come back in, say, an hour and a half?'

'How long do you think it takes me to get ready?'

It wasn't until he had grinned, said, 'Right, half an hour, then,' and left the room that she realised her indignation at his assumption that it took her so long to make herself presentable meant she had missed an opportunity to buy herself more time to recover from the way he was making her feel. Though she could have said three hours and probably should have said at least an hour, she had let him get to her and so he'd given her a tight timeline, knowing that she would be determined not to be a second late.

Walking across to the massive wardrobes, she focused on the positives—at least he wasn't going to sit there and wait—but she quickly met her second challenge…there appeared to be no handle in the smooth wooden surface. It wasn't until she inadvertently pressed her palm to a panel that the doors slid silently open, revealing a massive space.

The new items hanging in their protective covers covered a fraction of what was available, and she dropped to her knees to check the shoeboxes neatly stacked…still not sure if he'd been joking.

He hadn't been.

There were ten pairs of shoes, all in two sizes.

The clothes were all in one size—*her* size—and there was a bigger selection than many shops she knew carried. She didn't buy many clothes for herself normally, though she had an eye for a bargain and she knew what suited her. Ultimately, what she felt comfortable in was quite often plain old jeans and a T-shirt.

Neither was available, so after a short sift through Abby pulled out a pair of palazzo trousers with deep pockets in a subtle silvery blue and a square-shouldered fifties-style shirt in a slightly darker shade brightened by drifts of butterflies.

She used her bra and pants from her overnight bag, though a quick glance in one of the drawers in the antique chest revealed a vast selection of silky underclothes in mouth-watering shades and gorgeous fabrics.

She pulled out her one make-up bag from the hold-all and, after pushing her hair back from her face with an Alice band she applied that too. It didn't take long—just her usual moisturisers and sunscreen, a smudge of blusher across her cheekbones and a smudge of brown eyeshadow on her eyelids. She tended not to wear mascara as her eyelashes were naturally brown and long, though they never curled without a lot of encouragement. Finishing off with a defiant slash of bold red lipstick, she let her hair fall loose. Standing in front of the mirror, she subjected her wild curls to a wrinkle-nosed scrutiny. The time constraint ruled out straightening it so, after holding it on top of her head for a moment while she tried to figure out how to tame it, she released it with a hiss of dissatisfaction and delayed the decision by going back into the bedroom to dress. Sliding on a pair of low-heeled red mules, she went over to one of the full-length mirrors to judge the results, but before she reached it there was a tap on the door. The visitor didn't wait for a response, he just walked in.

The sardonic half-smile curling his mouth at the corners flattened out when he saw her and he walked across the room towards her. Abby was flustered by his sudden appearance but she still managed to notice the clenched tension below his relaxed exterior.

'I'm *nearly* ready.'

'Take your time…' His glance drifted upwards from her feet to the top of her glossy head, returning to rest on her lips. 'You look ready to me.' She looked incredible…like a classy, sassy female lead in one of the classic old black and white Hollywood movies his mother had introduced him to as a kid…elegant but sexy and in full, glorious colour.

She stuck out her chin. 'Are you trying to be funny?' She lifted a hand to her tumbling curls. 'I haven't done anything with my hair.'

'It looks fine to me,' Zain replied in a voice that gave no hint that he was imagining those curls falling down her naked back and over her breasts. It would cover them now it was inches longer than it had been ten months ago… He sucked in a sense-cooling breath through flared nostrils and pushed away the raunchy image. 'What do you still need to do?'

He arranged his long, lean length in a chair,

aware her resentment was growing and choosing to push her by adopting a bored demeanour.

'I need to make myself presentable...' She lifted the weight of her hair off her neck and let it fall back in a gesture that suggested it explained everything. For Zain, it explained nothing. 'Presentable for all those people who are probably lined up outside to look at me. Perhaps I should wear a veil...or would that offend people?' Looking suddenly and completely overwhelmed by what she'd signed up for, she grabbed the padded back of a nearby chair, taking a deep breath before adding despairingly, 'You see, I don't have a clue.'

His clicking fingers cut through her diatribe of complaint. He refused to believe that a woman who looked the way she did had any confidence issues. 'Do not play the victim, it doesn't suit you.'

This bracing and unsympathetic advice brought her chin up, a move he was growing used to very quickly.

'And it is also extremely unconvincing. I have seen you stand up to men wielding knives,' he reminded her. 'And as for presentable...presentable...' he parroted. 'What the hell is that?'

'It's something my nan always said before she left the house… *Do I look presentable?*' The mention of her grandmother brought a wistfulness to her face and she blinked to clear the tears he could see her fighting. Before he could say anything to try and help, a hopeful smile spread across her face.

'Perhaps your sister-in-law,' she began eagerly. 'Do you think if we told her the story she'd help me? I mean, it was her job, so surely she'd be able to give me some pointers.'

'No.' His emphatic response was designed to flatten her enthusiasm, and it worked.

'But—' she began to protest.

'You will not approach Kayla.' He moved towards her as he spoke, his voice not raised, but each ice-edged syllable had a dangerously explosive quality that was echoed in his body language; he looked big and dangerous.

Breath held, her hands tightened on the back of the chair, he wasn't sure if it was pride or paralysis that made her hold eye contact. It was definitely not good sense—that would have had her running for the nearest exit. Instead she tilted her head back, mirroring the tension he knew drew the skin tight across the angles and planes of his face.

He paused a few feet from where she stood

and added in the same soft, deadly tone, 'And you will not tell her our story.' He could only imagine what Kayla would do with that sort of information. 'Is that understood?'

'Well, I don't see what the harm would be,' she began mutinously.

'Stay away from Kayla, Abigail,' he intoned grimly. Seeing her opening up to Kayla, all earnest eyes and the best of intentions, would be like watching a kitten ask advice from a tiger. The image in his head was enough to make him break out in a cold sweat.

Refusing to categorise the feeling in his gut as protective, Zain zoned in on the practical measures he would need to put in place to protect Abby from Kayla, who would consider Abby, or anyone else that came between her and what she wanted, the enemy.

'Why?'

The question floored him but before he could think of a suitable response a look of comprehension appeared on Abby's face.

'Oh, God, I'm sorry, I wasn't thinking... you're right.'

Zain made a non-committal sound in his throat, glad she had reached the conclusion but not sure how she had got there.

'I wasn't thinking.'

Slightly thrown by her abrupt capitulation Zain watched her lips twisted in a self-recriminatory grimace.

'She must be devastated.'

'She is, I'm sure.' Though he imagined that fury was a more accurate description of Kayla's likely reaction to having her position at the pinnacle of society being taken from her.

'I won't bother her, I promise. It must be a terrible thing to lose your husband so young... I can't even begin to imagine.' She lifted her hand to her hair. 'Could you wait a minute while I tie it back?'

His eyes moved down the golden red waves. 'Your hair is spectacular just as it is.' It was no less than a statement of fact. 'And no one will be offended no matter how you appear—most women in Aarifa stopped wearing the veil a generation ago...a few of the older or more conservative do when they go out in public but it is their choice. So just relax.'

It took Abby a few moments to recover, not just from her reaction to having him call any part of her spectacular, but also to the flash of sense-incinerating fire she had seen in his eyes that had sent her heart rate crashing through the ceiling.

'Relax…?' She managed a laugh at the idea. 'I'm living in a velvet-lined box.'

'I can have you moved to another room.'

She gave a sigh of frustration. 'Not the room! I mean the *situation*. The lying and the money and—'

'Yes, I get it, but compared to escaping from desert pirates it should be child's play.'

'Pirates. I suppose they were, and the desert is a bit like the sea too,' she reflected, a little shudder tracing a path up her spine as she recalled the vast emptiness. 'I didn't escape. I hung on, that's all,' she reminded him, a glimmer of a smile tilting one corner of her lips as she recalled that journey through the blackness of the desert.

The memory reminded her too that she owed him, big time. He hadn't played that card, he even seemed inclined to play down the fact he had saved her from a fate that Abby considered worse than death. Given how much she owed him, he wasn't, when she really thought about it, asking so very much in return. So it didn't sit well with her conscience; being uneasy was not much to ask of her in the grand scheme of things.

'I signed on for this so don't worry, I won't wimp out.'

'I like your hair that way…it is you.'

Before she had the opportunity to decide if that had been a compliment or an insult he was opening the door for her to pass through. As she did he stopped her, patting his trouser pockets. 'I've forgotten my phone…hold on…' He paused. 'What are you scared of?'

'I'm not scared…just…people are going to be curious, to ask questions.'

'I feel confident that they won't, but if they do simply refer them to me.'

Her little chin lifted in challenge once more. 'I don't need a man to speak for me! Do you even know how sexist that sounds?'

'You were the one playing helpless,' he pointed out.

The term grated on Abby.

She glared at him through narrowed eyes. 'I wasn't playing.'

'So you are helpless, then?'

Her exasperated glare morphed into confusion when instead of moving past her through the door he backtracked, heading towards the row of cupboards that lined the opposite wall.

'What are you do…?'

She stopped, her mouth ajar, as he opened one of the doors and stepped through.

'What the…?' She followed him, pushing

the door wider and seeing that there was no closet behind it, there was another room. As she walked through to it, it became obvious that the room was a bedroom on the same palatial scale as her own but much more sparsely furnished than the one allocated to her and very definitely masculine.

She stood there, frozen in the concealed doorway, as Zain went to a desk on one wall and shifted some papers to find what he was looking for. It took her a few seconds for the significance to sink in. When it did she experienced a flare of alarmed fury!

'Got it!'

Her jaw tightened—*was that all he had to say?* 'This,' she said in a frozen voice, 'is a bedroom?'

'Hard to get anything past you.'

Her lips compressed. '*Your* bedroom?' she added, her voice heavy with accusation.

'Right again.'

Her chest swelled. 'Was anyone going to tell me that there was a secret door in my room?'

The conversational tone didn't fool him for a minute—he knew she was mad as hell and yet he appeared to enjoy watching her like this.

'Oh, it isn't a secret, *cara*, everyone knows it's there. My great-great-grandfather had it put in when he moved his favourite mistress into the palace. And as we are married it is almost obligatory to share the same bedroom suite, if not the same bed…' He paused, his gaze sliding down the long, supple curves of her body. 'Unless, of course, you do wish to *share*…? Relax,' he recommended before she could react. 'There's a lock on the connecting door. We can use it if you're worried about your virtue.'

His mockery stung colour into her smooth cheeks, or maybe it was the thrill of illicit excitement low in her stomach.

'I am perfectly capable of defending my virtue, thank you.' The question that was becoming more relevant, considering that even his voice had the ability to make her quiver, was, did she actually *want* to defend it?

She lowered her gaze as the internal admission brought a rosy flush to her cheeks.

'So I don't need a lock.' A bit of self-control might help though, she thought despairingly.

'I do not doubt it, but the lock is on *my* side.' The lock might be on one side but the attraction, the same attraction that had flared into life in the desert, was mutual, and stronger than anything he had ever experienced in his life.

If the circumstances had been different he would have enjoyed exploring it, and her. His chiselled jaw tightened as he reminded himself that they were to be together for eighteen months, and, while sharing sex might make the first couple of months easier and *definitely* more enjoyable, it still left the months that came after.

In his experience, when lust burnt itself out the very things that had attracted you in the first place became irritants, and then there was the boredom... Under normal circumstances the solution was walking away, but in this situation that was not an option.

Even this sobering thought did not stop his eyes making an unscheduled journey up the long, supple curves of her spectacular body once more, or the heat that pooled in his groin. Jaw clenched, he made himself walk past her before he did or said something he would definitely regret.

The lightning-quick return sliced through Abby's veneer of bravado.

'In your dreams,' she said contemptuously.

He swung back without warning, the speed and fluidity of his action taking her unawares. He was standing so close, towering over her, and he could feel the heat of her body. She reacted instinctively to the force of his sheer male physicality, placing her palms flat and pushing hard against his chest.

Her strength was nothing compared to his resolve and as her eyes became locked with his he slid a hand to the small of her back and pressed her against his chest, trapping her hands between them and doing nothing to hide his arousal.

She struggled for breath, the air emerging from her parted lips in a series of stressed little gasps. Zain was breathing hard too, his breath warm on her face as he bent his head until there were only centimetres of air between their lips.

The breathless stillness could have lasted a second or an hour before it was broken by Zain.

'You want to know about my dreams, *cara*…?' he said thickly. Alarm bells louder than those she had set off the previous day were screeching in his head but he tuned them out. This was just sex.

Abby moaned, her eyelids closing as he moved his lips across her own so lightly it was agony as every nerve in his body tensed and started screaming.

It was the little shudder, the warm lips that softened beneath his that cut through the last threads of Zain's control. He slid his fingers into her silky hair, wrapping them through the fiery strands and letting instinct take over as he kissed her like a starving man.

Abby responded to the searing contact, parting her lips under his probing pressure and welcoming the intimacy, craving it as she fell into the hard, hungry kiss.

They were both breathing like marathon runners when his mouth finally lifted. Warm breath mingling with hers, Zain stood there, his fingers tangled in her hair, the side of his nose resting against her own.

The muscles along his jaw quivered as he gently kissed the corner of her mouth. 'You want to explore my dreams a little longer? Or maybe your dreams…?'

'I don't have those sort of dreams,' she said.

CHAPTER ELEVEN

IGNORING HIS LOOK of disbelief, Abby barged past him and out of the door, mortified, ashamed by her response, but much, much more disturbed by the illicit excitement that remained low in her belly.

'So you've decided to take the lead?'

She flashed him a look of dislike. Her insides were trembling. He looked totally cool and she resented and envied his ability to turn his passion on and off like a tap as if it meant nothing to him.

It meant nothing to *me*, she added firmly to herself, and repeated it just to emphasise the fact—*nothing*. 'Are they going to follow us all the time?' she asked crankily.

He looked blank; he was actually struggling to focus. 'They who…?'

'The two large men with granite faces and… at a guess, automatic weapons over their shoulders, who are ten paces behind us. Is that ringing any bells?'

'Oh…you tune them out after a while.' It was that or go mad. 'Security.'

'I didn't think they were the entertainment… do they follow you everywhere?'

You could get used to anything, she supposed, even the low, disturbing electric thrum in the air when Zain was around…so long as she didn't touch him, she would cope.

'They try to.'

'It's very intrusive…'

'It's the art of living in a velvet-lined box.'

The reminder dragged a reluctant smile from Abby. 'A figure of speech. It's actually a very beautiful box.' They were walking under arches of marble embellished with intricate carvings. Beneath their feet was a mosaic made of bright blues and golds, the colours so intense it looked as though it had been freshly laid, but it had to be ancient.

'If you slow down you might actually get to see some of it.'

With a slight tip of her head she acknowledged his comment.

'Are you in much pain?' she asked.

'I'm on strong painkillers.'

She tilted her head to look up at his strong profile. 'But are you actually taking them?'

'I put my comfort ahead of my macho reputation.'

'Do you have a macho…?' She caught her breath and rushed across to the archway that had given her a glimpse of the vista that had stopped her in her tracks. 'Oh, my goodness!' She put her hands on the wrought-iron rail that came up to hip height and leaned out.

With a sharp admonition of, 'Careful!' he tugged her back from the railings embedded in the base of the opening that appeared to be cut into a single rose-coloured stone so massive it looked like a rock face.

It took several moments for Zain's heart to slide back down from his throat, where it had climbed, and into his chest—the image of her leaning out too far and simply falling out into space was hard to shake.

His chest continued to heave like someone who'd just had to sprint ten kilometres, his breath hissing out in fast, measured gasps, his bruised ribs screaming in protest. As he turned his head to study her profile she appeared utterly oblivious to the fact she had ever been in any danger, and utterly oblivious to him, her enraptured gaze fixed on the panoramic vista.

He'd wanted to surprise her, to see her re-action, but the plan had definitely backfired. He was the one who'd been surprised...and probably taken twelve months off his life in the process.

The original city had been built up around the palace on three sides, and this side faced the desert, the endless sand dunes rising organically from the rock of the building's foundations.

Nothing broke the undulating miles and miles of red desert until it reached the mountains, blue in the distance against the even more vivid, eye-aching blue of a sky that seemed to go on for ever.

Abby was so completely enthralled by the dazzling vista that it took her a few moments to register that Zain was standing behind her, his hand on her shoulders. As compelling as the view was, her appreciation was drowned beneath the awareness of his warm proximity.

She felt the shudder start in her toes and begin to rise... She stepped forward to break contact but instead his grip tightened and he swore softly as he turned her around to face him.

'For God's sake, woman, are you trying to

kill yourself?' Without taking his angry eyes from her face he jerked his head in the direction of the drop.

She frowned in bewilderment at his stressed exclamation.

'The drop is two hundred feet.' He spaced the words, enunciating them slowly through his lips.

Her expression cleared. 'Oh, I'm fine with heights.'

His chiselled jaw clenched. 'Well, I am not fine with scraping up pieces of your stupid—' He bit back any further remarks and shook his dark head, his big hands sliding downwards from her shoulders to her upper arms. He seemed at the point of jerking her towards him when instead he stepped backwards, releasing the breath that had clearly been trapped in his chest in a deep sigh.

Relieved there was a barrier of air between them, she might have been able to clear the whirling fog of emotions in her head if he hadn't continued to stare at her with daunting disapproval, mingled with something else she couldn't quite name.

The something else made her heart rate escalate, throwing the stressed organ against her ribcage as her eyes went to his mouth, remembering his kiss as she swallowed to relieve the contraction in her dry throat.

She didn't have a clue how long they stayed there, a frozen tableau, before he finally broke the silence, though not with a kiss this time.

'You scared me witless…this place—'

'It's beautiful.'

You're beautiful, she thought, unable to stop staring at his face.

He nodded. 'Yes, but it is also dangerous.'

So were the currents she could feel shimmering like silken ribbons in the air between them.

'My ancestors used to bring their enemies here and push them to their deaths…'

She gave a shudder at the image his words created in her head.

'When I was a boy I used to be fascinated by the gruesome stories in the way that small boys are always fascinated by gruesome anything. On my twelfth birthday, my brother said he had a present for me…he brought me here…' His head turned towards the ledge. 'By that time I was as tall as Khalid, but two of his friends were waiting. They held me over the edge and threatened to drop me…they wanted me to say my mother was a slut… I wouldn't, so they held me there until I passed out from fear.'

She hadn't felt dizzy standing at the edge but the furious reaction she felt in response to his matter-of-fact recounting of the story of bullying rose up in her now, so strong that her head spun. 'Oh, that's so terrible…wicked… no wonder you are scared of this place!' she exclaimed.

'I'm not scared of this place.'

'It's fine if you are,' she soothed, taking his hand as she began to back away from the stone opening.

It took him a moment to realise the astonishing truth: she was looking after him… With a twisted half-smile he allowed her to drag him away until she stood with her back to the wall and he was facing her a few feet away from the opening.

'Is that better?'

'I'm really not afraid of heights—my father cured me. Somehow, he heard about what had happened. I never questioned how, I just accepted his omnipotence.' There was a wistful edge to his soft laugh. 'Anyway, he brought me here and told me to look over the edge.'

She looked up at him, eyes wide with shock and indignation.

'That was brutal!'

She couldn't believe it when he shook his head in denial of her condemnation. He actually smiled, and the poignant quality of the motion made her ache with sadness.

'I refused point-blank and so he brought a stone out from his pocket. It was large, smooth and black.' He extended his hand, rubbing his thumb across his palm as though he was seeing it, feeling it there.

'A stone?'

'He gave it to me and told me that it was very valuable, he explained that it had magical qualities, that the person who carried it would never fall. He said it had been given to him by a famous climber who had conquered Everest.'

Abby's shoulders relaxed as she smiled. 'You believed him.' She was taken by the story and the image in her head of Zain as a little boy.

'I was still afraid of the drop, but yes, I believed him and actually more than that I didn't want to disappoint him. So every day we met here and each day I looked over the edge with a little less fear than the previous day. After a week of coming here, only to have my father not show up, I got bored and curious so I took the stone from my pocket and climbed up onto the ledge. Did I mention I was a rather curious child? I wondered what would happen if I dropped it…so I did.

'When I turned around my father was standing there. I told him the stone hadn't worked. It had fallen.'

'And what did he say?'

'He just shrugged and said, "Yes, but you didn't." And walked away.'

Abby smiled at the story. 'It sounds as though you had a great relationship.'

'When I was a child, certainly.'

'But not now?' Even before his expression froze over she was regretting her probing. 'I'm sorry, it's none of my business.'

'Why not? It is no secret.' He turned away to stare out of the window, his face in profile remote, his voice devoid of expression as he continued. 'My father was a good man, and at one time a good ruler. He was strong, everyone respected him and the people worshipped him. When I heard the stories of the early days of his rule I wanted to be just like him.'

His bitter, reflective laugh made her wince. 'What happened?'

'There was an enormous scandal when he married my mother—she had a past and he had a wife, Khalid's mother. But he didn't care; his *love* for my mother was an obsession, a *dis-*

ease. He put his personal happiness ahead of his duty.'

'Maybe,' she began tentatively. 'He felt he needed the woman he loved beside him to do his job as ruler?'

He whipped around, his mouth twisted into a sneer as he responded to her softly issued suggestion. 'She left him!'

'And you,' she said, her heart aching with compassion for the boy he had been and sad for the man he had become, a man who seemed to have sealed himself off emotionally.

'I survived but my father did not—he went to pieces, he cared about nothing…his duty, this land…and he would take her back tomorrow if she would come.'

'Poor man…' A little shudder ran like a chill down Abby's spine; it must be terrible to love someone you couldn't have…to taste a little of paradise and be thrown out.

'*Poor man?*' Zain's nostrils flared in outrage at the suggestion. 'He is a leader, a ruler, he has responsibilities—the people, the land relied on him and he left them. Oh, he is still here physically, but he might as well not be.'

'You're angry with him?' Her heart ached for the little boy discovering his hero had feet of clay. His determination to stay single and his contempt for marriage certainly made sense in light of the family history he had revealed.

'I'm ashamed of him.' The words were wrenched from somewhere deep inside him and he seemed almost as shocked to have said them as she was to hear them. Zain turned abruptly away, obviously regretting that he had confided so much in her…and disturbed that he had.

'Are you coming? We have a lot of ground to cover,' he said in a clipped tone as he strode away.

She nodded quickly and ran to catch him up.

He was right, there was a lot of ground and all of it was the stuff of superlatives. Zain spoke of geometric patterns and symmetry but to her the corridors and courtyards, the ballrooms and paved quadrangles had no logical sequence. It was a beautiful, glittering maze, but Zain was a good guide—he didn't try and overwhelm her with too much detail but instead told her little snippets, gossipy stories that made his ancestors seem very real people and not just the daunting historical figures in portraits that lined the gallery above the ballroom with its mirrored, domed ceiling of blue glass.

But, as fascinating as the stories he told were, Abby could not stop thinking about the present-day story, the sad, tragic tale of his parents.

'Now, this,' he said as they walked along a wide corridor with a vaulted ceiling, 'is the oldest part of the Palace complex. You won't come this way unless you're going to the stables.'

Abby had fallen a little behind and stopped. 'Do you think they will ever get back together?'

Zain inhaled, his nostrils flaring as he turned around to face her.

She stood her ground while his gaze swept across her face. 'Your parents?' she pushed out nervously.

'You like a happy ending?' he sneered.

She gave a little shrug, wishing she had kept her mouth shut. 'Doesn't everyone? Don't you think you would be happier if you could forgive your father? He couldn't help falling in love.'

His jaw clenched before he responded. 'While I am grateful for your unsolicited wifely concern for my welfare,' he told her with blighting insincerity, 'it is not required. You are my wife on paper only, so please don't get carried away by the job description.'

She breathed through the utterly irrational hurt that quivered through her body. 'I'll do my level best,' she promised before miming a zipping motion across her lips.

He said something not in any language she understood before some of his rigidity fell away and something approaching a smile twisted his lips. 'You, silent? That I'll believe when I see it. But for the record you are wrong, you *can* help... Falling implies a helplessness that does not exist; there is always a choice.'

She searched his lean face for any sign of doubt and found none at all; he radiated male arrogance. Her insides shuddered, the mouth-drying sensation dramatic and disturbing as she continued to stare at him.

Always a choice, she mused; well, she had one now: carry on looking and feeling like this or look away; argue or bite her tongue.

She chose the latter in both cases, probably the way to go for the next eighteen months.

'So this leads to the stables,' she said.

'Yes,' he said, experiencing a sense of anti-climax as he let her walk before him under a large stone arch guarded by massive, double-metal-banded doors and into the fresh air.

Abby took a deep breath and took it all in,

turning her head towards the sound of thundering hooves as a string of horses with riders on their backs galloped out through the open gates. They left behind a hum of activity she hadn't yet experienced in Aarifa.

She had encountered a few people during the tour but all had bowed to Zain and scooted out of their way, so their functions in this vast complex had not been immediately obvious to Abby.

Here was different, with everyone occupied on a specific task, be it grooming one of the horses, mucking out stables, leading horses across the cobbled yard or walking them into what seemed to be a horse bath.

'Hydrotherapy,' Zain explained when he saw her staring. He took her arm and steered her towards the nearest row of stables; there were three similar rows that lined three sides of the quadrangle, while the fourth seemed to house offices.

'I know that horses are not your thing, but I thought you might like to say hello to an old friend.' He took her across to a stable door, pausing to speak to one of the stable hands with a lack of formality that surprised Abby.

The young man moved ahead of them, tipping his head towards Abby as he passed. As they reached the stable he had gone inside he emerged leading a horse.

'Malik al-Layl,' Zain said, taking the ends of the reins from the stable hand and leading the stallion towards Abby. 'I think he remembers you,' Zain said as the horse snickered and put his head down towards Abby, who, after a self-conscious moment of indecision, extended her hand towards the animal.

'We were not formally introduced, Malik...' She glanced towards Zain for guidance.

'Malik al-Layl—it means King of the Night.'

'We were not formally introduced, Malik al-Layl, but I don't blame you for that.' She shot a look loaded with meaning at Zain. 'There was a lot of anonymity going on.' She jumped as the horse brushed her hand with velvety lips, her smile spreading. 'I think he *might* remember me,' she said, unable to hide her pleasure at the thought.

'Once seen, never forgotten.'

Their eyes met and the *something* that she had sensed earlier—the crackly charge she had been conscious of several times—surfaced once again. She lowered her gaze quickly but it still hung there in the air as she pretended to look for something in the pocket of her trousers and watched covertly as Zain ran his hand down the stallion's flank, the dangerous male aura he exuded sending little thrills through her nervous system.

'Lost something?'

Like someone caught in the act…well, in some ways, she had been lucky her sin remained in thought and not in action, and Abby pulled her empty hand out of her pocket.

'I was just looking for a tissue…' she improvised. 'I'm fine.' The hasty addition was just in case he decided to send for someone to fetch her a gold-lined box of the things.

'I was wondering if you'd like to have some riding lessons while you're here?'

'You make it sound as though I'm on holiday.'

'It doesn't have to be a punishment—there is nothing that says you can't enjoy yourself.' His eyes connected with hers, the teasing look making her feel warm and *other things*. 'You might even get to like me…'

Her half-smile flattened as she realised that was the problem, the one she didn't want to acknowledge—that it might be far too easy to like him. 'That's pushing it,' she husked out, refusing to analyse why the idea scared her so much. 'But I would like to learn to ride.'

'Fine, I'll…' He broke off, his eyes moving

past her in response to the sound of the clatter of hooves.

Abby turned her head, curious to see who had galloped through the gates just as the rider of the first horse dismounted. As the woman landed with almost balletic grace, the two men who had ridden in behind her shadowed the move but with far less elegance.

Before the riders had hit the ground, grooms were rushing up to take the reins of the horses.

The woman pulled off her riding cap and shook back a dark bell of smooth, shiny hair. She barely glanced at the man who took it from her hands then led away her mount, though she did call something out to the two men who were clearly her security detail. They bowed in response.

She then swung around and, shoulders back, head high, helmet in hand, with a swing of her slim hips she walked towards where Abby and Zain stood.

Abby looked towards Zain and found he was not looking at the tiny brunette but at her. He seemed to read the unspoken question in her eyes and nodded almost imperceptibly.

Abby put his tension down to a fear she was about to say or do something that would blow their cover. His concern, she admitted, was pretty well-founded.

'Zain, darling!'

For a moment Zain did nothing but then he took a deep breath, lifted his hand and walked out to greet the woman.

They met somewhere in the middle, close enough for Abby to see what the other woman looked like but not hear what they were saying apart from the odd word that floated out... which sounded French.

Abby wasn't prepared for the flood of peculiar emotions seeing them together released, rising to the surface like oil on water. She examined the woman rather than the feelings.

At a distance, there had been the suggestion of glossy perfection. Closer to, this was intensified; the other woman didn't have a hair out of place, literally. The dark hair that swung to her shoulders in a bell-like curve was smooth and glossy and there wasn't a single crease in the tight-fitting riding breeches that were moulded to her bottom and thighs or a mark on her whiter-than-white shirt. The knee-high riding boots she wore had a glossy sheen and clung to her calves, the darker, fitted jacket on top was nipped in where it buttoned at the waist and the scarf arranged artfully around her neck added the final chic touch.

In profile, her features looked small and neat, and next to Zain she was tiny and delicate-looking. She was just the sort of woman that brought out protective instincts in men.

The sort of woman who always made Abby feel big and clumsy. For a split second she was back at school, towering over the other girls, hearing the popular girls laugh and snigger at her in the hallways. Annoyed with herself, she forced the images away—she had moved on a long time ago, she reminded herself.

The sound of female laughter drifting across to her brought Abby's attention firmly back to the present and she found herself clenching her teeth, her curiosity turning to something else, something that made her want to look away, but she couldn't. She continued to watch as the woman reached out a hand and laid it on Zain's chest… Was the intimacy of the gesture a figment of her imagination?

She watched as Zain turned and gestured in her own direction—clearly he was talking about her, but *what was he saying...*? The woman turned too and, lifting a gloved hand, she waved. It took Abby a split second to respond with a jerky movement of her hand.

Then the couple began to walk towards her.

By the time they reached her Abby had a very creditable smile painted on her face.

'Kayla, this is my wife, Abby; Abby, this is Kayla, my…brother's widow.' Zain smoothly made the formal introductions.

Abby tipped her head, still in shock at hearing Zain call her *his wife*. 'I'm very sorry…for your loss.'

The woman's red lips stretched into a gracious smile, her mouth the perfect rosebud shape. Her diamond earrings flashed in the sunlight. 'Thank you. It has been a difficult time…my mother insisted I go out this morning; she knew that it would help. Zain understands. He feels the same way.'

It was hard to tell from Zain's expression if he felt anything at all. His expression was tight and stony.

Kayla clasped a hand to her chest. Not anticipating the dramatic gesture, Abby stepped back.

'The desert…for us…' Kayla's glance took in Zain. 'It is hard to explain to an outsider…it is an almost spiritual connection that cleanses the soul.'

Struggling to know what to say to this, Abby just nodded and heard herself say stupidly, 'That's nice.'

'I'm sorry I wasn't here last night to greet you.' Abby noted how the gracious smile did not quite reach her dark eyes.

'No…not at all,' Abby stammered.

'Everyone wants to meet you—perhaps we could have tea one day? Go shopping… I'm sure we will be great friends.' She leaned in and, stretching upwards, kissed the air either side of Abby's face. Abby's nostrils flared as she was engulfed in a cloud of exotic-smelling cloying perfume.

Without waiting for a response, Kayla turned and lifted her face to Zain.

Abby turned away, tangling her fingers in the animal's mane but aware in the periphery of her vision that the pause before Zain bent forward was one second away from being awkward. She didn't look as he air-brushed her cheek with his lips but turned in time to see the other woman catch hold of his hand, sandwich it between both of hers, the red nails bright against his skin, before pressing it to her chest and only then slowly releasing it.

There were tears in the corners of her dark eyes as she turned to Abby. 'Forgive me; it's just that I nearly lost both *my* men.'

Abby told herself she had imagined the em-

KIM LAWRENCE   195

phasis and nodded, feeling a little guilty that
her own sympathy felt so forced.

'Later, Zain...?' The tears dried as the beautiful brunette arched a brow in Zain's direction
and nodded to Abby before walking regally
away, the two men falling into step behind.

'So that is Kayla.'

'It is,' Zain agreed.

His response gave her no clue as to the cause
of the atmosphere she'd sensed between the
two of them. 'She's very beautiful.'

She's poison, Zain wanted to say. Instead he
gave the stallion one last pat and nodded to the
man who appeared to take him away. 'This
evening Kayla has asked us to join her for dinner.'

Abby nodded but with little enthusiasm. 'It
must be very hard for her.'

'I said you were still too tired.'

He was giving her an out but he fervently
hoped she wouldn't take it.

'Will you be all right?'

'Why wouldn't I be all right?' Abby asked
in confusion. 'It's not as though we're going
to be living in each other's pockets, is it? I'm
sure you're going to be busy getting used to
your new role...'

He tipped his head in acknowledgement. 'I do intend to be more...hands-on than my brother. It will be a steep learning curve. Concerning your days, things will run smoother once you have a team of staff around you. I have selected some candidates but I wasn't sure of you'd like to interview them personally or have Layla or one of my team do it?'

'Staff...team...me...?' She shook her head in an attitude of bewilderment.

'Obviously you will have your own staff.'

'But surely that wouldn't be necessary—I'm not really—'

He cut across her faltering protest. 'The world is meant to think you are *really*, and what do you intend to do for the next eighteen months—hide in your room? You'll be bored stiff in two minutes,' he predicted.

'So you want me to fill my time with riding lessons, and what, unveiling statues, general good works...?' The barely disguised uncertainty in her voice told him she didn't have a clue what the royal duties of the wife of a prince were.

'It might keep you out of trouble.' And hopefully out of Kayla's way. The only reason he had accepted this evening's invite was to make it quite clear to Kayla that she was to keep

away from Abby and to dash any expectation
she had that the two of them would ever get
back together.

The memory of her propositioning him in a
not very subtle manner he assumed had been
meant to arouse him, with his wife standing just feet away, was still fresh in his mind.
The effect on him had been the opposite to
what she'd intended, as Zain had stood there
wondering, as he did now, how he could ever
have been taken in by her, how he could have
missed the naked ambition that motivated her.
His response to her inappropriate overture had
been constrained by the public place; this evening it would not be.

CHAPTER TWELVE

IT SEEMED TO Abby that Zain took a more direct route back to the suite; he appeared lost in his own thoughts and to such a degree that she was struggling to keep up with the pace he set. So after a couple of attempts to break the silence she gave up.

At the door to her room he paused, seeming to notice for the first time that he was a little out of breath, and glanced at the metal-banded watch on his wrist.

'Sorry, I'm late. I have an appointment with my father.' He added, evidently feeling guilty he was leaving her alone, 'Layla will be available if you want anything.'

She nodded absently, still absorbing the fact that she was living in a world where you made an appointment to see your father.

About to turn away, he swung back. 'He lives quite a secluded life and my brother's death has hit him hard, so don't take it personally if he doesn't want to see you.' He sketched a forced smile that left his eyes sombre and shadowed. 'I never do.'

She watched him stride away, tall and powerful, wondering if he'd told himself the same thing when he was a little boy who'd needed his father.

Abby spent some time responding to texts from her grandparents and a much longer one from her agent, who wanted to know where she was. She ate her supper in the small private sitting room, preferring it to the dining room—which had all the intimacy of a banqueting hall—before sinking gratefully into the scented water of a warm bath. She closed her eyes and floated but the calm she sought eluded her, her brain continuing to fire off in all directions, thoughts and questions swirling in her head.

How had Zain's meeting with his father gone—was the sheikh angry that his son had been secretly married? Was Zain telling Kayla all about it over dinner? Was she making him feel better? Abby couldn't figure out if she had imagined or over-egged the intimacy she sensed between Zain and the widow…in Abby's head she had become the *black* widow, thought that might have just been her jealousy talking.

'Jealousy!' she yelped out loud, sinking under the scented water before coming up gasping and spluttering a second later.

'Do not go there, Abby,' she told her fogged reflection in one of the many mirrors. So yes, she *was* attracted to Zain—all right, *attracted* didn't really cover it… Zain had woken up a dormant sensual side of her that she hadn't even known existed—but she couldn't lose sight of the fact that she was here to do a job, a job that meant they spent a lot of time together in close proximity. But she would be vigilant not to confuse that closeness with real intimacy and in eighteen months she was out of here.

Easing herself out of the warm water, she scrubbed the mist off the mirror and pushed the wet hair back from her face. 'Do you want sex if it's just cheap and meaningless?'

It kind of depends on who's offering it…

Her eyes widened before she closed them with a groan. Sometimes honesty was definitely *not* the best policy. Standing up, she reached for one of the neatly folded bath sheets, muttering, 'Just as well he's not offering,' and keeping her eyes on the floor as she padded back through to the bedroom, afraid the mirrors might evoke some more unwanted insights. She just had to keep reminding herself that she was here to provide a smooth transition of power and nothing else.

The two men who had shadowed him at a respectful distance stopped when Zain halted and waited. It was the fourth such pause he had made since he left his father's apartments, still in a state of shock. As he walked past the two uniformed guards who flanked the entrance to his own private section of the palace he nodded to the men behind him, who peeled away as he shut the door.

He leaned against it. Zain was not a man easily shocked but he was… He closed his eyes as the relevant section of his conversation with his father continued to play on a loop in his head.

'Several members of the council have come to me to express their…concern over this marriage, and your choice of bride.'

Zain, who had expected this, had only half listened while his father recited the names, and none had surprised him. But then his father had said something that *did* surprise him.

'I told them that you have my total support.'

Zain had not doubted his ability to gain his father's support by appealing to his sentimental nature, but to receive it totally unprompted had surprised him.

'I am glad you have found someone,' his father had continued. 'Leading this country can be a lonely job and it's not one I would inflict on my worst enemy, let alone my son, without a great deal of thought.'

'It will not be my job for a long time, Father.'

'It will; I intend to step down and let you take control, Zain. It is something I would have done sooner but your brother…well, let us not speak ill of the dead.'

Repetition did not lessen the shock value, Zain realised as he began to pace the room.

He had never needed a shoulder to lean on or someone to confide his fears to—there was no one in his life to let him down, to leave. But both his father and Abby had spoken about the loneliness of the role.

To Zain, being alone was a positive, but it was not a point of view he imagined he stood any chance of converting Abby to—she rather unexpectedly turned out to have a romanticised view of life which even a profession not known for sentiment had not knocked out of her—and she was stubborn.

One corner of his mouth half lifted as, in his mind, the lines of her face quivered and solidified, becoming so real that for a moment it was as if he could reach out and touch her, but when he blinked and his vision cleared there was just the door she lay behind.

He walked across to it, hand outstretched, only to let it still on the heavy handle for a long time before he dropped it back to his side and walked away, reminding himself that alone was an *advantage* not a disability.

Unlike the previous night, Abby *didn't* fall asleep the moment her head hit the pillow—she tossed and turned as her thoughts went around in dizzying circles, bits of conversation from the last couple of days drifting through as her mind disconnected thoughts and images.

Occasionally her eyes would go to the hidden door to Zain's rooms as she wondered about past times when it had been used for illicit liaisons, about the mistresses and wives of powerful men who had lain in this bed before her, though she was not a mistress…and a wife in name only.

A wife who frequently felt as if she were the only twenty-two-year-old virgin on the planet. It wasn't deliberate; in her teens she had been the butt of male jokes—too tall, too thin, too gawky…too weird—so she had focused on her books and read about true romance. Not the fumbling sort her contemporaries boasted of enjoying, but grand passions, soulmates.

The irony was that now, even though she was essentially the same person, she had plenty of men lusting after her, to the point that she'd had to adopt an aloof reputation to put them off. The last thing she actually wanted to be was untouchable so Abby had decided she was setting the bar too high, which was the reason she'd taken a chance on Greg, working on the theory that, while he didn't set her on fire, she recognised the strong possibility that nobody would, and he was so nice—irony didn't get much darker really.

Maybe it was an evolutionary process and she was a slow starter; she had found unrequited lust now—and frankly she wouldn't have recommended it to anyone—so maybe one day she might discover what love felt like too…she just hoped it was better than this!

This reflection drove her from her bed. Barefoot, she walked across to the windows. She hadn't closed the curtains—there was no one to see in, considering her room and the entire private section belonging to Zain was situated in one of the highest of the three towers the palace boasted.

She could see the paved herb garden far below, the fragrance drifting up on the warm night air, the sound from the series of fountains a distant trickle. It was soothing and as she lifted her face towards the warm breeze it caught the folds of the nightdress that she had taken from the selection neatly folded in one of the drawers; soft chiffon silk in a pale shade of blue, it reached mid-calf and gathered under her breasts. One of the ribbon straps slipped as she pushed her hair back from her face.

She froze, one hand pressed to her head, fingers deep in the lush red curls, the other hand on the intricate wrought-iron rail of the Juliet balcony, as a disturbing sound broke the dark silence.

The sound was almost feral…an animal, perhaps, but what sort of animal would be roaming the palace grounds at night? Then the terrible lost sound came again. It was not, she realised, coming from the grounds, but from the room next door and from the throat of a person.

She didn't think, she just raced to the secret door and rushed through. Like her, Zain had not closed the curtains. The moonlight was streaming into the room, giving the illusion that carved wooden bed in the centre of it was spotlit.

The feral-sounding wail that emerged from the figure in it sent a chill through her blood. Heart pounding, she raced across the room and, climbing onto the bed, crammed forward to kneel beside the hunched figure on his knees, the tangled sheet over his body covering him only to waist level, leaving his head, his heaving shoulders and back exposed to the moonlight. The skin gleamed like oiled gold as every individual muscle tensed, tautly defined like an anatomical diagram displaying the perfection of the human form.

The only sound now, to her relief, was Zain's laboured dragging in and sighing out of deep, drowning breaths and the heavy thud-thud of her heartbeat as the blood pounded in her ears.

'Zain...?'

His head lifted fractionally at the sound of her voice. 'Go back to bed, Abigail,' he shook out in a muffled, raw voice that pained her ears like nails on a chalk board.

It was good advice and she knew it.

She reached out, hesitating a moment before she touched his shoulder and felt his muscles tense in rejection. Under the slick of sweat his skin felt cold to the touch.

'Get the hell out!' he growled.

Logic said she should do just that, but in

the same way as her physical response to him was something elemental, the response to his obvious suffering was equally instinctive and strong. It went beyond empathy and easily drowned out the voices of self-preservation in her head.

She tucked her legs underneath her and sat there. 'Well, you can be as rude as you like, call the guards to cart me off to the dungeon if you want, but I'm not moving until you tell me what the hell was going on—that was no dream, that was...' She thought of the nerve-shredding sound and shuddered. 'You might as well talk to me. I'm vastly cheaper than a therapist and my confidentiality is guaranteed.'

After a moment he sighed and flipped over onto his back, eyes closed. In the moonlight the angles and planes on his face took on the aspect of a beautifully carved statue.

The seconds dragged and his silence continued to contrast with the emotions she could feel rolling off him.

She could see the waistband of a pair of boxers just below the crest of his hip bone, his belly flat and ridged, showing each individual muscle with every inhalation. The multicoloured bruises down one side of his ribcage and upper torso shone through the light triangular dusting of body hair on his chest. His body had a power and beauty that dragged an emotional response from some previously unknown portion of her heart.

'Go away, Abigail Foster. I am not...*safe*.' His smoky blue gaze slid from her face and down her body, betraying the sinful thoughts in his mind.

He closed his eyes as if fighting against a surge of primal possessiveness.

'I'm not prying... I just want...' she began, framing her words carefully before stopping and straightening her shoulders. 'I just want to help and it's no use trying to scare me. I'm not afraid of you.'

His eyes opened and she nodded, smiling serenely down at him as she realised that she was telling the truth. She never had been afraid of him—even that first time when she had not known if he was one of the good guys, she had felt safe with him.

'Is it the accident? Is your memory coming back?'

He huffed out a dry laugh. 'It never went away, *cara*.'

'I know you said you didn't get on with your brother.' Her lips tightened as she recalled the dead man's idea of a birthday present. 'But you *were* brothers…and I know that people feel guilty when they survive and—'

He lifted a hand and touched a finger to her lips.

Abby inhaled and forgot what she'd been about to say as a deep tingle surged through her body from the point of contact.

He took the finger away and she breathed out, watching as he curved his arm on the pillow above his head; the stretch involved a contraction of muscle that inflamed the tingling she was already feeling inside.

'I am not suffering survivor guilt…surviving is my way of…' He broke off, as if at a loss to explain his relationship to someone like her. 'I wish the world were the way you think it is, *cara*—you think that blood is thicker than water, but the brutal reality is that brothers do not always love one another. Some brothers hate…my brother hated me.'

Assailed by a sense of helplessness, she felt the lump of emotion in her throat swelling. She hated to see him hurting like this and beating himself up…guilty for something that no one could have prevented.

'You can't blame yourself, it was an accident, you argued…that is what families do—'

'I really don't feel guilty,' he cut back with

savage, biting emphasis that made her wonder if she was missing something.

'Well, then, that's good.'

'Good!' he spat before closing his eyes and clapping a hand heavily to his head. A moment later his hand fell away and he raised himself on one elbow, his free hand going to her chin, drawing her face around to look at him. 'The truth is it was no accident. It was planned.'

'How is that possible?'

'It's possible because…' He paused, a battle waging across his face as he struggled to force the words out. 'You have that wholesome, shiny, dewy-eyed belief that goodness will overcome, don't you?'

'I'm not that naive, Zain, but yes, I do think that if you give people a chance they will mostly do the right thing…yes, I do.'

'The *right thing*!' he echoed. 'Do you think it was the *right* thing that my brother invited me there that day with the intention of ending both our lives?' He must have heard her sharp intake of breath, seen her pale, shocked face, but he ignored both. 'Khalid had found out that his life was ending—he had terminal cancer, the autopsy after the accident confirmed it—and he decided to put his—what do they say?—yes, his "affairs" in order.

'He took great delight in telling me he was going to take me with him—his last revenge. Khalid's last *I love you, brother* moment.' His bitter laugh cut her like a shower of glass shards.

'It wasn't an accident.' Her horrified whisper sounded loud in the silent room. 'It was attempted murder.'

'And he very nearly succeeded. I would be dead if that door had not given at the last moment and every time I close my eyes I see my brother's face and know how much he hated me.'

'I'm so, so sorry. Have you told anyone?'

Something flashed in his eyes as he looked at her and shook his head.

Shock vibrated through him; he had never intended to share the knowledge with anyone, let alone a woman he barely knew. There was nothing between him and this woman except a sexual attraction, he told himself, refusing to examine the suspicious knot of emotion that lay like a lead weight behind his breast bone. She had awoken in him something stronger than anything he had ever experienced and for the first time he realised how some men mistook this sort of primal connection for love.

'My father must never know— it would... Khalid put him through hell over the years. I don't want him to know the truth behind his death…what my brother tried to do. It would kill him.'

She pressed a hand to her heart as though making a vow as she held his eyes and shook her head. 'I won't tell him… I won't tell anyone.'

Their eyes were locked, the silent, deep connection stretching as he reached up his long fingers, digging into the deep, silky mesh of waves at the back of her head.

Her heart thudding audibly, Abby rose up on her knees and placed her palms flat on either side of his head as he dragged her face slowly down to his.

The first brush of his lips sent a jolt of shock fizzing through her body. She tensed and then, with a sigh, relaxed into the pressure of his slow, seductive exploration. Her body arched over him as his hands slid down her shoulders, moving slowly over the thin silk of her nightdress. By the time they reached the curve of her taut bottom she was quivering with need.

'I have wanted you from the moment I saw you,' he said thickly, easing her onto her back and rising over her.

The raw desire in his voice excited her more than Abby would have believed possible. She ran her hands down his back—it was all hard muscle and silky skin—but stopped suddenly, remembering his injures.

In the act of sliding down her body he stopped and lifted his head. 'What's wrong?'

'I want you, Zain, I want to touch you... taste you...' She shocked herself with the bold admission before adding a half-whispered, 'I don't want to hurt you.'

His laugh held relief and warmth. 'Let me show how much you're hurting me, angel.'

He took her hand and fed it down his body, sliding it under the waistband of his shorts, watching her face as he curled her fingers around the smooth, hard shaft of his erection.

She gasped, her heart pumping as her smoky stare connected with his. The carnal image that flashed into her head of him inside her so hot and hard made her fingers tighten, and she felt rather than heard the feral moan that vibrated deep within the vault of his chest as he took her hand away and held it on the pillow beside her face. With his free hand he stroked down her cheek and, holding her eyes, slid one and then the other thin strap of her nightdress off her shoulders.

He leaned in close, his breath warm on her cheek. 'Your skin is like silk,' he rasped, pressing an open-mouthed kiss to the blue-veined hollow at the base of her throat. 'I want to see you.'

The erotic statement took her breath away and tightened the hard knot of desire low in her belly but also released a flicker of fear that spoilt the moment.

'What's wrong?'

'You do realise that my photos are air-brushed, right?' She looked at him through her lashes, her body language defensive as she pushed out, 'I'm not perfect...and I've never really felt this way before...'

He caught her two clenched fists and brought them up to his lips. 'You are beautiful.'

Her lashes lifted from her cheek.

'And I want... I *need* you.'

The raw, driven quality of his admission started to melt away her doubts and the hungry kiss that followed it completed the job.

She lay there breathing hard as he levered himself far enough away to pull her nightdress down to her waist. His eyes made her think of blue molten fire, and they left a burning trail on her skin as he hungrily absorbed her quivering breasts, cupping one in his hand. When he ran his tongue across the engorged peak, she stopped thinking at all.

It ought to have felt strange to be touched but it just felt gloriously right.

The sight of his dark head against her breast was the most erotic thing she had ever seen. When he lifted his head his cheekbones were scored with dull colour. 'I want to feel you around me, Abigail, holding me tight.'

She struggled to force her response past the aching occlusion in her throat as his words sparked a flame into life inside her. She had wanted him, wanted to give him comfort, wanted to feel it in return—to feel warm and safe—but this was not comfort, it was something hotter and more dangerous, something wild. Her skin felt heated and she was shaking with need as he caressed her breast once more, and then, as she moaned against his mouth, he took hold of the fabric bunched at her waist and pulled.

There was a jagged tearing sound and then a moment later cool air was on her hot skin.

She opened her eyes as he levered himself away and pulled herself into a sitting position, but the protest in her face faded away when she saw he had only left her to kick away his shorts.

As he turned back to her, her greedy glance slid over the strong, perfect contours of his body. The power and the beauty of his fully aroused male body made her head spin with desire that thudded like a hammer in her head and pooled hotly between her legs.

A hand on her breastbone, he pushed her back down and brought his hands to either side of her face as he covered her body with his.

The first skin-to-skin contact of their naked bodies was electric. He parted her lips and sank his tongue deep into her mouth, the repeated penetration a rehearsal for what was to come. Abby sank her finger into his hair and kissed him back with a wild, combative ferocity that matched his.

His hands were everywhere, touching her, caressing her until her pleasure-saturated nerves were screaming for some sort of relief.

When his hand slid between her legs, his finger spreading the sensitive folds and sliding into the warm slickness of her femininity, she screamed his name.

'Zain!'

Her fingers clawed his back as he parted her legs and mounted her, his powerful body, slick with sweat, rearing over her before he slid into her in one powerful thrust.

A slow sigh hissed through her parted lips as, head thrown back, she absorbed the sensation of him inside her, making her aware of herself in a way that she had never experienced before.

Her eyelids flickered as she heard the astonished growl of his exclamation, the words muffled as his head dropped into her shoulder, then lifting fractionally. This time she could make out what he was saying and hear the concern in his deep voice.

'Are you all right?'

All right? She was absolutely incredible! 'Better than all right,' she husked. 'Don't stop, please…?'

'I couldn't even if I wanted to!' The tension in the raw admission was mirrored in the taut, strained lines of his face as he began to move again, drawing a sigh of relief from Abby. The sigh of pleasure became something more as by slow, careful increments he sank deeper before pulling out, repeating the movement, touching places that fed directly to the pleasure centres in her brain.

Her back arching, she grabbed his hips, pulling him deeper into her. There were no barriers of any sort between them, there was no check on the things she said to him, the words she used to urge him on as she wrapped her legs tight around him and let him take her into uncharted territory with each stroke.

She reached the explosive climax a second after she felt his hot release inside her; every muscle in her body spasmed then relaxed, the process repeating until she lay spent and breathing hard, pressed down into the mattress by his weight.

She was still floating some place out of her body when he moved to lie beside her on his back.

A primal surge of possessiveness tightened in Zain's chest, the powerful, fundamental response interwoven with tenderness as he struggled with the realisation that he had been Abby's first, her *only* lover. Something he hadn't thought possible.

'I lost control… I'm sorry.'

The words were heavy with self-recrimination and Abby's head turned sharply towards him on the pillow, their glances locked.

'Take that back,' she hissed furiously. 'Don't you *dare* say you're sorry.'

'I assumed…there is a lot of stuff out there about—' It was no excuse and he felt ashamed for voicing it.

'My multiple lovers? None of it is true—it

was only ever my agency trying to get publicity. I've never even met some of the men I'm meant to have been sleeping with—one of them is even gay, though I don't think he actually knows it yet.'

'And you don't mind?'

'It's mostly harmless, and Nana and Pops don't do the internet or read tabloids so there's no harm done.'

'If I'd known you had never been with a man before I would have not been so—'

'You were perfect,' she cut in, blushing ferociously.

'I would be flattered except you've not really had any other experiences for comparison, have you? Another thing...' He hesitated.

'I'm fine. What did I do wrong?'

'Not you, me... I... I didn't use protection; are you...?'

She shook her head. 'No.'

'Right, that could be a complication.'

She swallowed. 'It was just one time.'

He reached for her and pulled her down to him, a realisation dawning on him—the possibilities this new development created. 'It doesn't have to be one time...eighteen months is a long time to go without...'

* * *

Abby could have pointed out that she had gone twenty-two years *without* with no ill effects, but she didn't. Shading her eyes with her lashes, she asked, 'So does that mean you won't be...?' She broke off, arching her back as he ran a hand over the curve of her bottom.

Zain completed the question for her. 'Sleeping around?'

An image of Zain in bed with faceless and beautiful women floated into her head along with a stab of pain that felt as if a hand had reached into her chest and squeezed hard.

Abby looked away and nodded, hoping nothing in her expression gave away the fact that his reply mattered more than a little to her.

'I have too much respect for you to do that.'

She didn't doubt his words but there was a certain uneasiness in his tone.

'I don't want your respect, I want... I want...' Shaking her head, Abby struggled to sit up but was prevented by the weight and tensile strength of the arm that lay across her shoulders.

A long finger on the angle of her jaw brought her face around to his, her lashes lowered before he could read the answer to his question in her eyes. 'Abby, *what* do you want?'

'I want…' It was as if someone had turned up an invisible volume control and the whisper that had been active in the back of her mind became a loud, deafening and infinitely shocking shout.

Love!

She wanted love!

A strong sense of self-preservation made her rush immediately into rationalisation mode— of course she wanted love; didn't everyone? Only a fool would fall in love with a man who didn't believe in love…a man who had to all intents and purposes walled off his own feelings. But could she really walk away from what Zain was offering after she'd experienced a passion more intense than she had ever thought possible? Love was wonderful but there was also something to be said for a physical connection that defied explanation.

So maybe this was nothing more than strong sexual attraction—*very* strong…primal even— amplified by their first dramatic meeting and the fact she had just made love to the man who had haunted her dreams ever since he rode to her rescue. From a safe distance she could call it temporary insanity, but there was no reason to call it anything else now, not when she could embrace the opportunity Zain was giving her and enjoy the situation as it was.

Her muddled thoughts were interrupted as he kissed her, his lips warm and persuasive, moving over her body. Suddenly none of the questions seemed to matter so much. She would take what was on offer!

'I want this too…' he said against her mouth. 'Besides, I'm not about to give grist to the rumour mill by taking anyone other than my wife to bed, especially considering the new developments.'

'What new developments?'

'My father told me tonight that he intends to abdicate in my favour. I persuaded him to wait before he announces anything, but eyes are going to be watching me very closely once this leaks.'

Which, of course, it would.

'That means you're going to—' The rest was lost in the warmth of his mouth.

'Be very frustrated,' he rasped against her lips, 'if you don't focus on the next lesson.'

His voice in the semi-darkness made her shiver. 'There's a next lesson?'

It turned out there were two more that night.

CHAPTER THIRTEEN

ZAIN HAD LEFT before she woke. She had a vague memory of him kissing her goodbye, but that must have been hours ago, as the bed beside her was now cold.

It wasn't the first time Abby had woken alone since she came to Aarifa and she never liked it, but during the last four weeks she had come to realise that Zain worked harder than anyone she knew.

Having a greater grasp of Aarifan politics after four weeks of immersion therapy on the subject, Abby understood why he worked as hard as he did. He had no choice.

At first Zain had seemed surprised by her questions and Abby suspected he had initially doubted her interest was genuine, as his early responses had been pretty monosyllabic, but as he'd come to realise that her interest was real he had opened up and become more expansive. Now it had reached the point where he volunteered information—be it a breakthrough or an obstacle—without actually waiting for her to ask.

A couple of times recently he'd even asked her opinion. It gave her a little glow to know that he valued it, or, at least, it seemed he did to her.

But they never discussed the widowed princess, Kayla. Over the last few weeks malicious rumours had started to spread, which as far as Abby could make out were intended to harm her reputation. Luckily, the wife of a courtier she had become friendly with had warned Abby that it was Kayla spreading these, and Abby had been able to minimise the damage. There were also rumours that Zain and Kayla had once had a relationship before Kayla's marriage, which had made Abby burn with jealousy. When she had asked the woman why Kayla hated her so much, she'd needed pushing but had finally expanded on her initial diplomatic, *It's not my place to say.*

'Kayla wants what you have, Amira. I went to school with her, and she will do anything to get what she wants. Tell the Prince,' she'd said.

But Abby knew Zain would only tell her to stay away from Kayla. And, besides, she wanted to show him she was strong enough to confront this on her own. It certainly wasn't her place to be jealous of whatever might have happened in the past. Nevertheless, it gave her comfort to know that every night it was *their* bedroom Zain came to.

Sliding out of bed, she headed for the bathroom, humming softly under her breath, but she stopped humming when she became aware of the familiar monthly ache low down in her belly. Since that first night they had slept together they had been careful to use protection, but a tiny part of her had been nagging at her, aware there was some chance she might be pregnant. But now, the evidence to the contrary was clear and suddenly overwhelming.

Without warning, the tears just kept coming, gushing out from some unidentified region deep inside her, before finally they dried to an occasional burble of misery. Sniffing, Abby walked across to the marble washbasin and turned the cold tap on full, telling her red-eyed image sternly to, 'Get a grip!'

She splashed her face with water and switched off the tap but stayed where she was, leaning on the basin, looking at herself, a questioning frown furrowing her smooth brow.

Her reaction had been inexplicable, and not just the reaction but also the strength of it.

This was a good outcome, the *desired* outcome, she reminded herself. She knew that, and yes, she *was* relieved, or at least part of her was. But there was another part that felt oddly…what…? *Bereft.* The recognition deepened her frown and increased her growing sense of unease.

She hadn't wanted to be pregnant—it would have complicated an already complicated situation and she'd been too scared to even imagine the consequences of an accidental baby, considering their arrangement. Not that the idea of pregnancy scared her; she wanted a child one day but she wanted that baby to be the product of a loving relationship. She wanted to give the man she would eventually love in a 'forever after' sort of way the ultimate gift of his child.

Another sob began working its way past her trembling lips but it never escaped. Instead her eyes flew wide and she literally stopped breathing, the blood seeping from her face and leaving it paper-pale!

The truth hit Abby with the force of a tsunami blast and continued to reverberate through her body: some secret part of her *had* wanted a child because she loved Zain!

Because she *did* love him. As the denial fell away the pain rushed in to fill the vacuum it left. Loving a man who would never return those feelings was always going to hurt, which was why she supposed she had been in denial, filling her thoughts with enough irrelevant chatter to drown out the words that were now shouting inside her head.

Zain was the last man she would have expected to fall in love with. No matter what he said, Zain was wrong—there was no choice involved; love defied all logic.

Patience was not one of Zain's strengths and Aarifan politics seemed a slow-moving machine. The past few weeks had been at times incredibly frustrating—there had been moments when he had struggled to retain control in the face of the obstacles being put in his way by the powerful politicians who opposed his reforms in any and all ways they could.

But today had been a good day and it was still early, he saw, glancing down at his wrist. The early breakfast meeting had been an unexpected breakthrough. He had brought a previously obstinate opponent around to his way of thinking and he was buzzing with a sense of purpose.

It took days like this to keep him going through all the days when it felt as if he was being blocked at every turn, days when progress seemed impossible and the tightrope of diplomacy slippery as ice. Days when, if it wasn't for the fact he vented in private with Abby, he might have been tempted to forget the advent of civilisation and throw the whole avaricious bunch in a deep dungeon. Abby had proved a very effective sounding board, listening to him rage and talking him down.

She was going to be thrilled when she heard about this advance…he couldn't wait to— His footsteps slowed, a thunderstruck expression crossing his face…

He couldn't wait!

It was literally true.

He wanted so badly to share the victory with Abby, just as he had shared the defeats and setbacks, and it was something he could not imagine feeling a few short weeks ago.

How far had he strayed from his original game plan…what had it even been? He had rewritten the rules to fit the circumstances and his needs so often it was hard to remember. It was easy to justify his first diversion from the plan because it had been totally unrealistic to expect to fight the intense sexual attraction between them. He couldn't get enough of her and actually he couldn't even see why it had ever seemed so important to take such a masochistic stance, why he had seen danger where in fact there was pleasure.

Sex he could rationalise; what made him more uneasy was the recognition of the emotional, almost symbiotic, connection they seemed to have developed...if this was how he felt now, what was it going to be like when the eighteen months was up?

He made himself walk slowly to the door. It wasn't as if he needed her here; she liked to be involved...she was lonely, and it would have been cruel, he told himself, to leave her to her own devices.

Surely the only thing that had changed was that in eighteen months' time they would part as friends...if ex-lovers *could* be friends. Or maybe they would even be parents...that circumstance still an unknown, the memory of their first time and his thoughtlessness always there in the background.

He walked into Abby's room, almost tripping over the suitcase by the door.

For a split second shock closed his brain down—it closed everything down—then, as the paralysis weakened, something close to panic tightened like an icy fist in his belly. Before he identified it as such it shifted into full-blown, mind-numbing fury. She was running away. She was leaving him.

Didn't everyone?

He was literally shaking as he strode across the room and through the door between the wardrobes that lay open.

Passport in hand, Abby was standing looking adrift, the long, lightweight trench coat she wore open to reveal a plain white silk shirt she had teamed with dark, narrow pedal-pushers.

'What the hell is going on?' Had she intended to slip away while he was absent?

Abby blinked; she was working hard at disguising her misery, at the truth she was sure was written all over her face, and it left little or nothing to register his awesome fury.

'Sorry, it was a last-minute decision.' She managed a smile...held it for a few seconds before it faded, too bright and too brittle. Hell, she really needed some time to sort herself out—if she stayed now she'd do something irreversibly stupid like blurt out the truth. 'I would have rung but I didn't want to disturb your meeting...how did it go?'

'To hell with my meeting!' he growled.

'Sorry,' she said automatically, assuming from his attitude that it had gone badly. A knot of protective anger tightened in her chest; he worked so damned hard and for what seemed to her very little thanks. Sometimes she wished she could bang together the heads of those men making his life tough. 'It's just I've been putting off going to see Nana and Pops but I need to; I only told them half the story and they deserve more, plus the solicitor says the vendors are finally ready to exchange contracts, and I'd like to give them the keys in person.'

'You're coming back…' The wildness died from his eyes as they swept her face, and his body began to unclench as the explosive tension lowered. For the first time he noticed her pallor, the red rims around her beautiful eyes… the protective swell in his chest so intense it was a struggle to breathe past.

'Well, not tonight…unless you need me to?'

'I'm fine,' he said with a shrug that made it clear he didn't need anyone.

'The plane is on standby; I hope you don't mind,' she said, not quite meeting his eyes.

He frowned and she worried he could see through her lies.

'Of course not. You'll ring me when you land…?'

She nodded. 'Of course.'

'Come here…'

She went to him and sighed as he drew her body against his, smoothing her hair back. With one hand he cupped her chin and drew her mouth up to his… The tenderness meshing with the passion brought an emotional lump to her throat.

Afraid she was going burst into tears, she pulled away, sure that if she lost control she might start blurting out things she shouldn't. She allowed herself to say 'I love you' silently in her head but kept her mouth closed.

Zain didn't want her love and he certainly wouldn't have wanted their baby. But she had, she really had. Until this morning, she hadn't known just how much that hope had flickered inside her.

Hand on the door handle, she turned back. 'Oh, and I'm not pregnant, by the way, so you can relax.' She managed what she hoped was an unaffected laugh before she almost threw herself through the door because this time no amount of determination could stop the tears.

A few days later as Abby returned to Aarifa the sadness was not gone but it was contained.

Although she had told herself otherwise, she knew that she had allowed herself to hope.

It had been a selfish thing, wanting a child that was a bit of Zain because she couldn't have him or his love. She recognised that now. A baby should have two parents who loved one another…it didn't always happen, of course, but in a perfect world it would, and didn't everyone want their child to be born in a perfect world?

She had to focus on what she had, not what she didn't have. Her chin lifted as the co-pilot came out to ask her if she'd had a good flight and then continued to make small talk while she only half listened. She would make some lovely memories over the next few months, memories to treasure when she returned to her old life, not that it would ever be the same, she realised, because *she* wasn't the same.

It was weird stepping off the plane and walking into the wall of heat that not long ago had felt so alien but now felt like home.

Bubbles of excitement exploded like star bursts in her stomach as she shifted in her seat, leaning forward to stare out of the window as first the city gates came into view and then the palace.

She had told Zain that she would be back

late-afternoon but she planned to surprise him with an early arrival, telling the palace staff to keep quiet. Although, she realised now, it might not be much of a surprise if he was tied up in meetings all morning.

Quietly entering the sitting room, which was empty, she moved through to the bedroom they shared. It was empty, the bedclothes rumpled, which was surprising, considering how keen the housekeeping was under Layla's watchful eye.

Ah, well, at least Abby would have time to repair the ravages wrought by the flight. Dropping her handbag, she walked across to the bed, automatically twitching the quilt to pull it into place. As she did so, something glittered as it fell. Abby bent to pick up the small, shining object and as she lifted it her heart stopped.

She had seen the very distinctive diamond earring before, she realised. Kayla had been wearing it that first day in the stables. A whimper escaped her white, clenched lips.

The hand she pressed to her mouth to contain further cries shook; she shook everywhere as she stared at the tiny object that had shattered any and all illusions she had built up about how Zain might really feel.

She couldn't be angry that their marriage

was a sham—it was *meant* to be a sham—but she could be angry and hurt and mad as hell that he was a cheat!

She backed away from the bed, unable to bear the things she saw when she stared at it—her bed, their bed…it felt like a violation that he had taken *her* to their bed…maybe not even for the first time.

'Oh, excuse me… I am so sorry.'

Wiping her eyes with the back of her hand, Abby spun around to see a young woman in the uniform worn by the household staff standing there.

The girl dropped a curtsey. 'So sorry to disturb you but I…' She saw the diamond sparkling in Abby's hand and exclaimed. 'Oh, you have found it! I am so grateful.'

Smiling, she went to grab the earring out of Abby's hand but Abby's fingers closed over it. There was something strangely familiar about the girl.

'It is a very pretty thing,' Abby said, realising where she had seen her before—at Kayla's side on those rare events when their paths crossed.

'It's not real but it was a gift. I am most grateful—it must have come out when I made the bed.' The girl held up a hand with a look that was probably meant to feign innocence but was hampered by the hint of a smirk.

Maybe it was the smirk, the connection to Kayla, or maybe just the fact she was able to think past that first blast of hurt, jealous outrage, but suddenly Abby joined the dots and saw what this was about…

So… Kayla wanted Zain, the crown or maybe even both. It had been obvious from the rumours that Kayla didn't like her, but Abby had told herself that it didn't matter, she was not here long enough for it to matter, and she had no intention of running to Zain any time she had a problem. She had wanted to prove to him she could cope.

She had been wrong not to tell him. This was a problem that needed addressing immediately.

'No, I don't think that's what happened at all.' What was Kayla's problem? she wondered, watching the look of revealing shocked apprehension wash over the girl's face. 'Where is Kayla, your mistress? I think I'd like to return this trinket.' She dangled the earring. 'In person,' she added grimly.

The girl looked scared now and as Abby walked towards her she shadowed the steps, backing towards the door. 'I… I don't know, really—the stables maybe, Amira?' She fled.

When Abby reached the stables a stable hand she recognised spotted her and approached shyly.

'You want to see the King of Night?' he asked in halting English.

To Abby, her King of the Night would always be Zain. 'Yes, please, if it's not too much bother?'

The idea of anything being a bother seemed to shock him.

Abby fingered the earring in her pocket. 'Have you seen the Princess Kayla?'

'She was here, Amira, but she left.'

Abby was not sorry to hear this; her appetite for a confrontation had waned considerably as she had walked the corridors. Wasn't there a certain amount of hypocrisy in her reaction? The woman might be trying to break up Abby's marriage but that marriage was a sham. 'Your English is excellent.'

He flushed with pleasure at the compliment. 'I worked in England long time ago at a very important race stable; it was my wish to be a jockey.' He pressed a hand to his stomach and rolled his eyes. 'But I got too fat... I like my food too much.'

'Well, the stables here are beautiful, spotless, and the weather is a great deal better than in England.'

'It is a very grey place,' the man agreed. 'But I enjoyed the fish and chips. Here he is.' He gestured towards the next stable along the row, one with the top door open.

The stallion whinnied as she approached.

'Hello, boy,' she whispered as she pressed her face into his mane.

'He likes you.'

Well, at least someone does, Abby thought, swallowing a sob of self-pity just as the person she least wanted to see in the world at this point appeared.

Not dressed for riding today, Kayla was instead wearing a pencil skirt that ended mid-calf, her legs elongated by the spiky heels she wore. Her silk top had bell sleeves and a square neck above which she wore some massively impressive pearls.

She lifted her chin; this woman was a bitch, but Abby's childhood experiences meant she had had a great deal of practice dealing with mean spirits and she knew that you should never let them see that they had got to you, as fear and pain were the food they fed on.

'Kayla.' She tipped her head in cool acknowledgement and had the satisfaction of seeing an expression of annoyance in the other woman's dark, malicious eyes as the thundering sound of horses being put through their paces on the gallops in the distance got louder and then faded away.

'How was your trip to England...*home*? You must miss it.'

'I miss my family and friends.' But not as much as she missed the sound of Zain's voice, the touch of his hand...his lips.

'Then I am surprised your visit there was so short.'

Abby closed her eyes and shook her head. She had no appetite for the cat-and-mouse fencing. She heaved out a long, sibilant sigh, opened her eyes, lifted her chin once more and prepared to take the metaphorical gloves off.

'Actually, I was looking for you. I think I have something of yours.' She held out her hand, the diamond stud between her fingers catching the light.

The woman's smile was almost as insincere as the sympathy and regret in her response.

'Oh, dear, I wouldn't have had you find out this way for the world.'

Abby's brows lifted as she dropped the earring onto the woman's palm. 'Find out what? That you are totally desperate and wouldn't know a moral scruple if it bit you?'

Kayla's triumphant smile faltered as her lips compressed in a petulant pout, but she recovered quickly and threw out a fresh taunt. 'You probably don't know, but I had a relationship with Zain before you were married.'

'I was here about five minutes before I learnt that on the palace grapevine.'

'But what you didn't know is that it carried on…and is *still* carrying on,' Kayla added before dramatically producing the twin to the earring.

Abby felt a fresh stab of shame for those split seconds when she had allowed her own insecurities and jealousy to make her jump.

'If you expect me to believe that you slept with my husband last night, forget it… Zain has too much…' her lips quivered and her eyes misted '…too much respect for me to act that way.' She clung tight to this; she might not have his love but by his actions Zain had proved time and time again that it wasn't just words—he did respect her.

The other woman's eyes flashed with pure malice in response to the simple pride ringing out in Abby's confident statement. 'You mean you amuse him right now. It won't last, you know; the novelty value will wear off.' Abby's dignified silence seemed to enrage the woman even more as she snarled out contemptuously, 'You love him, I suppose?'

'Yes.' Even in this situation it felt liberating to be able to say it out loud.

'And you think he loves you…? I suppose it is his great *love* for you that will carry him through the latest polling disaster…' She saw the flicker of shock in Abby's eyes and nodded. 'Oh, yes, not good news at all, but then, no great surprise either,' she drawled. 'His advisors were expecting it; they warned him that seeing you, an *outsider*, with him will always remind people of his mother.' She stepped in closer. 'You're the kiss of death for Zain, and if you really loved him you'd leave!' she hissed, before turning and sweeping majestically away.

Abby stood perfectly still, her thoughts whirling. Kayla was trying to manipulate her but that didn't mean what the woman was saying didn't have an element of truth—more than an element, she realised; it *was* the truth.

Presumably at the outset Zain had calculated that any damage to his reputation that the sham marriage to her might cause could be rectified after they split up down the line, but what if he was wrong…? What if the longer she stayed the more damage she did to his reputation… what if it became irreparable? What if the people he loved rejected him?

She knew that would kill him.

'Amira?'

The young stable boy was standing there looking concerned.

Abby shook her head and turned, pride keeping her head up as she walked away, her firm tread contrasting with the awful icy chills running through her body.

Her chaotic thoughts chased around in her head. She didn't know where she was going or what she was going to do yet she knew she needed space…time…distance…but a moment later the stable hand caught her up.

'Excuse me, Amira, but the driver found this in the car.'

She looked blankly at the tiny charm that had fallen from the bracelet that had been her mother's. 'Oh, thank him…' A sudden thought occurred to her: if she was going to do this it was best to do it quickly, better for Zain. 'Is the Prince here in the palace?' she asked quickly.

'Yes, I think so, Amira…'

Abby reached into the pocket of her trench coat, her fingers curling around the passport she had not removed.

'Do you have paper…a pen?'

Zain stood there for a full ten minutes after he had read the note.

He didn't trust himself to move.

She was gone; the note, the ink blurred, was some drivel about leaving for him…she had left!

He had never chased after a woman in his life and he wasn't about to now.

Last night he'd lain awake longing and aching for something he could not name that she gave him, missing her softness, her scent, her warmth.

But life was a hell of a lot simpler without her. Without her there was no temptation to allow her to do to him what his mother had done to his father. His mother had drained his father, making him grow weak, making him love her so much that she blocked out his responsibilities…to his people and to the son who needed him.

He couldn't silence the counter-argument in his head.

Had Abby made him weak…? Could he have done what he had done these past weeks without her support? She didn't take from him, didn't drain him. She gave instead.

And now she had gone.

The thoughts tumbled in circles around his head until he took a deep breath and blinked like a man waking up and realising he had one more shot. He hit the ground running.

Considering she was not exactly inconspicuous, it took him a long time to find anyone who had actually seen her. It took him fifteen minutes to track her as far as the stables and another five to discover that she had been seen deep in conversation with Kayla, after which it seemed she had been driven away.

A phone call to the private jet confirmed his suspicions. He made it clear that under no circumstances was the plane to take off, and went around to the garages.

His fastest car got him as far as the palace gates, where he found his way totally blocked by a hundred or so banner-waving protestors taking advantage of the fact that such gatherings were no longer prohibited—one of his reforms that had definitely backfired!

Frustrated but not defeated, he flung the high-powered car into reverse and drove back to the stable yard.

He saddled the stallion himself with stable hands watching and wondering who knew what? Zain didn't actually care—the burning frustration that drove his every action was choking him.

'Shall I stop, Amira?'

Dragged from the depths of her despairing reflections, Abby looked up. It didn't matter how many times she told herself her life was not over, it felt as if it was and so she could only try to take comfort from the fact she was doing the right thing. Maybe this knowledge would make her feel better in the future but right now it didn't.

'Pardon?'

The driver nodded to the rear-view mirror and Abby turned to see what he was looking at. The blood drained from her face and her heart began to thud as fast and hard as the hooves of the stallion that was galloping full pelt towards them.

'No!' she said in a wobbly voice of panic. 'Don't stop!'

'Amira!'

'Don't stop for anything!' she ordered imperiously as Zain and the stallion began to overtake the car.

'Yes, Amira.'

He did, of course, but he didn't really have a choice when there was a rearing stallion in the road ahead, the hooves inches away from the car bonnet.

'Sorry, Amira.'

Abby barely heard as she watched as Zain, looking just as rampantly male and awe-inspiring as the first time she had seen him, dismounted and walked over to the car.

He wrenched open the door. 'Get out, *cara*.'

She thought about ignoring the order but decided getting out of her own volition would be more dignified than being dragged out, and Zain looked more than capable of that.

While she stood there he leaned into the cab and spoke to the driver, who turned the car around and drove away before her horrified eyes.

Leaving her, Zain, the stallion and a lot of sand.

'Just like old times,' he said, walking towards her with long, purposeful strides.

She shook her head. He was standing almost toe to toe with her and looking at her in a way that made Abby's head spin as she looked up into his dark, lean, beautiful face, her heart lurching wildly in hope.

'What is this about, Zain…?'

'This.' He took her by the shoulders and dragged her into him, covering her mouth with his. The kiss went on and on.

When it stopped she stood there feeling quite crazily bereft.

'That doesn't change anything, except fine… Oh, God, I have no self-control when it comes to you! I'm just—'

'In love?'

She froze and thought, *Am I that obvious?* 'I wasn't trying to fall in love…'

He brushed a strand of hair from her cheek, the action so tender that it brought tears to her eyes. 'I know… I was actively fighting it…' A grin split his lean face… Suddenly he looked younger. 'I was a fool. It feels great to surrender to you.'

Golden joy burst inside her but she shook her head. 'You can't stay married to me.'

He looked at her with frustration. 'Are you going to tell me why?'

'The polls.'

'What polls?'

She gritted her teeth; he really wasn't making this easy for her. 'You don't have to pretend,' she said, wishing that doing the noble thing felt less absolutely awful. 'I know that the numbers were bad.' Her carefully composed voice acquired a little wobble that required her to stop and swallow several times before she continued, looking up into his face through a glaze of tears. 'I know that the longer I stay the worse they will get...the people will reject you because I remind them of your mother. So, I'm going now before things get worse, and don't try and stop me,' she warned, knowing that if he did she wouldn't have the strength to do the right thing.

He didn't look at all impressed by her sacrifice. 'Who the hell has been filling your head with this nonsense?'

'Kayla. And it's not nonsense, it's the truth.'

His expression darkened. 'Kayla...is poison.' He dismissed the other woman with a contemptuous click of his long, expressive fingers. 'The woman wants power and position. She had an affair with me to get it and, when I didn't play the game like she wanted, she married my brother. I should have kept her away from you. I thought I had; I'm sorry, *cara*.'

She knew she shouldn't but she leaned in

as he stroked her cheek, the tenderness in his face bringing tears to her eyes. 'The poll...'

He sighed. 'There was a poll, not instigated by me,' he added. 'And the numbers were not good but that was when the news was first broken. Another, this time with my approval, was put out in the field yesterday and the results came back this morning.'

Abby closed her eyes. 'I'm so sorry, Zain.'

'My popularity ratings have soared, all thanks, it seems, to my redheaded wife.'

Her eyes flew wide. 'Kayla lied!'

He arched a sardonic brow and drawled, 'Now, there's a shocker.' All hint of sardonic humour vanished as he framed her face between his hands. 'You're the dream I never even admitted I had, Abby. The dream I was afraid of. I've been a coward, and my only excuse is that I've been guarding my heart so long that I forgot I had one, and I was too cowardly to admit what I felt...felt from that first moment I saw you...so brave, so beautiful, so...'

She raised herself on tiptoes, grabbed his head and kissed him. The kiss led inevitably to another then another...and by the time they surfaced the horse had wandered a few yards away.

'Does this mean…?' Was it possible to explode from sheer happiness? She felt as though she was walking on air as light as the bubbles of happiness popping in her bloodstream.

'Yes?' he prompted.

'You want me to stay longer than eighteen months?'

'I want you beside me every day…' His voice dropped a shivery, sexy octave as he whispered, 'Every night,' against the sensitive skin of her earlobe. He stopped nuzzling her neck and lifted his head to stare down into her face with an expression that stopped her heart as he caught her hand and pressed it to his chest. 'I want you beside me always. I love you and I could not do this…any of it, without you.'

What could she say to that? With stars in her eyes Abby linked her arms around his neck. 'You saved my life; I think I owe you mine.'

'I don't want your gratitude, Abby. I want your heart, your love.'

She looked at him with shining eyes and whispered, 'You have both.'

Zain's eyes blazed with love as he took her hands and pressed them to his lips. 'I will keep them safe, I promise.'

Abby lifted her face to his kiss with a blissful sigh. 'I'm going to have to learn some languages.'

'The language of love is the only one that counts,' he said, leading her by the hand to the horse. Heaving himself with no seeming effort into the saddle, he held out a hand, which she took. A moment later she was sitting in front of him.

'Are we going home?'

'I like the way you say that, but no, I thought we might detour. There is a certain oasis I know.'

The wind caught her hair and whipped her laugh away as he kicked the King of the Night into a gallop across the red sand. It felt as though they were the only two people on earth and she liked it.

* * * * *